Cole's gaze flew to their entwined hands—his all but disinfected and Charlie's grimy.

Her touch shouldn't have any effect at all on him, but it did. A tingling, shocking, surprising effect.

It made no sense.

If there was one thing Cole knew about himself, it was that CJ—Charlie—Larson wasn't the type of woman he was attracted to. He dated sophisticates. He did *not* date towheaded tomboys who trained horses, had callused hands, drove beat-up pickups and who dressed no differently than he did when he was in his work clothes. No way.

D0367112

Books by Kate Welsh

Love Inspired

For the Sake of Her Child #39
Never Lie to an Angel #69
A Family for Christmas #83
Small-Town Dreams #100
Their Forever Love #120
The Girl Next Door #156
Silver Lining #173
Mountain Laurel #187

*Laurel Glen

KATE WELSH

is a two-time winner of the Romance Writers of America's coveted Golden Heart Award and a finalist for RWA's RITA® Award in 1999. Kate lives in Havertown, Pennsylvania, with her husband of thirty-one years. When not at work in her home office, creating stories and the characters that populate them, Kate fills her time with other creative outlets. There are few crafts she hasn't tried at least once or a sewing project that hasn't been a delicious temptation. Those ideas she can't resist grace her home or those of friends and family.

As a child she was often the "script writer" in neighborhood games of make-believe. Kate turned back to storytelling when her husband challenged her to write down the stories that were in her head. With Jesus so much a part of her life, Kate found it natural to incorporate Him in her writing. Her goal is to entertain her readers with wholesome stories of the love between two people the Lord has brought together and to teach His truths while she entertains.

Mountain Laurel
Kate Welsh

Love Inspired®

Published by Steeple Hill Books™

STEEPLE HILL BOOKS

ISBN 0-373-87194-5

MOUNTAIN LAUREL

Visit us at www.steeplehill.com

Printed in U.S.A.

And Jesus said, "Abba, Father, all things are possible for You. Take this cup away from me; nevertheless, not what I will, but what You will."

—*Mark* 14:36

A great big thank-you to Dr. Lise Lund
of Danville Animal Care Center, Equine Services,
for all her help with the treatment of encephalitis
and West Nile virus. Any errors are certainly
not hers, but mine. A doctor I am not!

To my daughters.
May you find God's will for your lives.

Prologue

He couldn't believe he was center stage at a wedding. Cole Taggert hated weddings. He hated commitment. Thankfully it wasn't his—wedding or commitment.

He might be thankful, but he wasn't happy. He hoped the smile he'd been practicing for days hid his feelings well. He'd known he'd feel this way, but one of Amelia's there'll-be-a-price-to-pay glares had him accepting as graciously as he could when his father asked him to be his best man at their wedding.

Now, he watched that same sweet woman, Amelia Howard—soon to be Mrs. Ross Taggert, mistress of Laurel Glen and his stepmother—glide into Laurel House's sunroom adorned in silky white that the November sunlight made look like whipped cream. She looked every bit as lovely and feminine as she was. But he'd seen her inner strength. She was the embodiment of a steel magnolia.

It wasn't that Cole wasn't happy for them. Amelia was a wonderful, compassionate woman who deserved a man like his father. And his father deserved a little happiness after years spent alone living with undeserved guilt over his first wife's death.

Cole knew his problem. He was jealous. Because though he hated thoughts of marriage and commitment, he also longed for the security and companionship he knew they could bring. His sister was married to and gloriously happy with his best friend, Jeff Carrington. And his father was so happy it hurt to look at his perpetual grin.

Cole heard a sniffle and glanced at his aunt Meg. Well, she was alone, but at least she had memories of love. One so special that in thirty years she hadn't found someone to replace her fallen soldier.

And that, in a nutshell, was his problem. Try though he had, Cole just couldn't give his love to any of the women he'd been involved with. He'd wanted to. He really had tried. But in the end he had broken their hearts because, no matter what, he couldn't commit his. Sometimes he wondered if he even had one.

Cole watched Amelia take her place next to his father. His sister, Hope, stepped up to take the bride's small, elegant bouquet. Now there were two women deserving of love. As a familiar thought raced through his mind, Cole felt his stomach flip then harden with the paralyzing fear that held him imprisoned. He'd always joked that if he ever met a woman like his sister, he'd run the other way.

The truth he'd never admitted to himself until that moment was that he wouldn't run out of aversion. He'd flee in fear. Because that was the kind of woman he could fall in love with. The kind he now avoided at all costs. The only kind who could reach his heart.

The only kind who could break it.

Chapter One

Cole squinted against the glare of the afternoon sun bouncing off the March snow blanketing the fields. Just ahead, at the top of the next rise, sat the boxy shape of a horse trailer pulled to the side of the road. He wondered if it was a neighbor or some guy bringing his horse to Laurel Glen.

When he got within thirty yards of the vehicles, Cole decided it had to be one of the older residents on the other side of the road who were barely holding onto their land in the face of the county's rising taxes. No one who owned this beat-to-death blue and rust trailer would be able to afford Laurel Glen's boarding fees, that was for sure.

He considered the near freezing temperature and the windchill factor of this mid-March day and pulled over behind the trailer. He was only three miles from Laurel Glen, the horse farm that had been in his family since the land grant days at Pennsylvania's inception. He couldn't help with car trouble, but he could change a tire or give some old guy a lift.

"I'd really better stop," Cole told his female companion. "He may need help."

She chuckled, a light, sexy sound that had no effect on him at all. Elizabeth Boyer was a beautiful woman, but she was his friend, and that's all she'd ever be. They were in agreement on that. He knew her from when she was the ugly duckling in a beautiful family, and she'd known him during what his family now kindly called his rebellious period. Neither was any good at relationships, so they kept each other company and held loneliness at bay.

"What's so funny?" he asked.

"You. I don't think I'll ever get used to this new community-conscious Cole Taggert. But then, you always were a softhearted pushover."

He winced, then laughed as he opened the door and stepped to the ground. "Hey," he said, grinning. "Don't spread it around, okay? You'll ruin my hard-earned bad-boy image."

Cole left Elizabeth laughing and rounded the back of the trailer. With no small amount of confusion, he took note of the championship lines of the magnificent palomino mare moving restively inside. The decaying trailer and the quality of the animal didn't jibe. And the guy's once-red pickup was in even worse shape than the trailer!

When Cole got a look at the owner hunkered down next to the front of the pickup, expertly spinning off the lug nuts with a cross jack, he stopped dead in his tracks.

This was no guy.

She was dressed exactly as he was. Worn jeans, work boots, a sheepskin-lined denim jacket. Other than the coat, her only concession to the weather was a pair of earmuffs.

He felt a smile tip his lips. She reminded him of his sister, Hope, before the awakening of her feminine side last year. This woman was every bit as young as Hope and just as petite in stature. Like his sister before her makeover at an all-day spa, this young woman's long shining mane of hair was pulled into a single thick braid that hung down the middle of her back. The only difference between the two was that the stranded motorist had hair as golden as the afternoon sunlight.

"I was going to offer to help," he said without preamble as the last lug nut came off, "but it looks as if you've got everything in hand."

She turned toward him and stood, her golden-brown eyes widening in surprise at finding him standing there. "Is that how it looks? Believe me, I don't. I used my spare ten miles ago when the driver's side front blew out." She bent to heft the heavy tire and wheel off the pickup.

"Uh-oh. That's not good," he commented, trying to decide why she made him nervous. She was certainly no threat, nor did she look in the least criminal.

"You have *no* idea how bad. Could you tell me how far Laurel Glen is from here?" She leaned the tire against the hub and swiped at her forehead with the back of her hand, leaving a streak of dirt behind.

"Another three miles. Are you boarding your mare at Laurel Glen?"

She chuckled at his incredulous tone, causing Cole to take a step back. Maybe Elizabeth didn't affect him, but this little ragamuffin certainly did. Deciding the unseasonable temperatures had frozen his last brain cell, Cole put the thought aside and laughed at her knowing smile.

"Sorry. It's just that Laurel Glen's fees are, ah…"

"Out of my league," she said. "You'd be right. Morning and I will be living there. I signed on as their new trainer."

Cole could only stare. This was the elusive trainer his father had been waiting for? This was CJ—Charlie—Larson? No way! It couldn't be. Even though Hope had been the last to hold the position for any length of time, and she'd done an exemplary job, his father would never hire a female as the new trainer. It wouldn't matter that he was desperate after two men hadn't worked out. Ever since Hope had located the new trainer, Ross had referred to CJ Larson as the new *man*, the *guy* due to arrive at any time.

But Cole was just as sure there hadn't been a mistake. Ross was expecting Charlie Larson, male. Hope and Jeff had apparently pulled a fast one by hiring a woman. Cole nearly laughed out loud imagining Ross's reaction to yet another female taking over as trainer. This was going to be too good to miss.

"Now there's a coincidence," he said unable to

keep from grinning. "I just happen to be headed that way and I picked up a can of instant flat fixer just last week. Suppose we put the tire back on and see if it'll get you there. You can follow me. You've only got another three miles to go."

"That's great. Thanks. I'm running so late already. I told Hope Carrington I'd get there at noon."

Why did her wide smile make the day seem brighter? "So, ah…" He hesitated, driving the thought away, and forced himself to consider the situation. "She planned to be on hand to welcome you?" Cole felt his grin widen. He was sure his cagey little sister had planned just that. There was no way she would let her precious new hire bump into their father unprepared for his reaction.

CJ stared at him for a long moment then blinked. "Hope said that was her plan. Is there a problem?"

"What was Hope's plan?" Elizabeth asked as she rounded the front of the trailer.

Cole turned and held her hand as she carefully stepped over the tongue and hitch. "Elizabeth, this is CJ Larson," he said, unable to keep from comparing the two women. Though both had been blessed with natural blond beauty, Elizabeth was a perfectly faceted jewel, and CJ was a diamond in the rough.

CJ stepped forward, extending her hand to Elizabeth in a gesture of friendliness. Elizabeth took it in the same spirit. Unfortunately, CJ's hand was still filthy from removing the tire. She grimaced, as did Elizabeth, when they both glanced at their joined hands. CJ quickly apologized, and Elizabeth waved it off as unnecessary.

"There's nothing but a few tumbled down places between here and Laurel Glen. What brings you all the way out here?" Elizabeth asked, her hand tucked behind her back. Cole wanted to laugh at the sight of her acting as if her hand hadn't become contaminated when she clearly felt it had.

"CJ is Laurel Glen's new trainer," Cole told his friend instead of razzing her for her prissy ways. "I was just telling CJ I was sure Hope had planned to be there to introduce her to Ross."

Elizabeth's eyes widened. "Undoubtedly," she said. She'd obviously caught his meaning.

This was going to be interesting. And it would have been funny seeing his father outmaneuvered if CJ Larson weren't about to get caught in the middle.

"So you think your plan will work?" CJ asked, looking back and forth between him and Elizabeth.

Plan? He didn't have a plan to convince Ross to keep her on. Not yet anyway.

"I don't mind telling you I wasn't looking forward to leading Morning down the road to Laurel Glen while I rolled the tire along," CJ went on, calling him back to the problem at hand.

"I doubt that will be necessary. Cole can call ahead for help on his cell phone if your tire won't hold air," Elizabeth assured her.

"I guess you two know the Taggerts and the Carringtons pretty well." CJ suddenly seemed uncertain.

Cole chuckled. "From the day Hope was born, and Jeff probably from the day I was." He put out his hand to shake hers. "Cole Taggert at your service."

"Oh. You're Hope's brother. The vet. She told me you live at Laurel Glen."

CJ reached out, took his proffered hand and froze, her eyes widening as their hands joined. Cole, too, went still at the zing he felt as his hand engulfed her work-roughened one. His gaze flew to their entwined hands of its own volition. Her touch shouldn't have any effect on him, but it did. A tingling, shocking, surprising effect.

It made no sense.

If there was one thing Cole knew about himself, it was that CJ—Charlie—Larson wasn't the type of woman he was attracted to. He dated sophisticates like Elizabeth Boyer. He did not date towheaded tomboys who trained horses, had callused hands, drove beat-up pickups and dressed no different than he did in his work clothes. No way.

He forced himself to let go and dismissed the reaction. It was impossible. Snapping out of his reverie, he narrowed his eyes in suspicion. Was Hope pulling one over on Ross or was she matchmaking again with her brother in mind? If she was, he'd put a stop to it real quick!

"Why would my sister mention me? I live there but I don't work there exclusively. I have my own practice."

She swiped at a loose tendril of hair blowing across her face and left yet another copious strip of dirt. Why on earth would that add to her appeal?

"I was a little uncertain about leaving my regular vet behind, and I worried one around here would cost more than I can handle. Hope told me Morning's vet fees would be part of my salary and that you have a wonderful reputation as a vet."

Cole nodded and smiled. He'd been foolish to forget that Hope knew him too well to think CJ Larson would interest him. That couldn't be the reason she'd been hired.

"I'll thank my sister for the compliment when I see her. Right now, though, I think we should get you back on the road so Morning can meet her stable mates."

CJ Larson climbed behind the wheel of her trusty pickup and breathed a sigh of relief. She blew on her cold, stiff fingers, supremely grateful to be away from Cole Taggert. He had to be the best-looking man she'd ever met. Or at least noticed. It wasn't just his features, which were admittedly male-model perfect. Or his hair, dark as sable, and eyes nearly the same shade. Or his wide-shouldered, narrow-hipped, long-legged physique. She supposed it was the whole package, topped by his lady-killer grin, that had gotten to her. Cole Taggert was one dangerous man for a woman's heart.

CJ couldn't remember ever feeling such instant attraction to anyone. She found the new and incredible feeling, and him, a bit scary. She'd thought this kind of attraction couldn't happen, that the sort of thing she'd felt at his touch was a myth perpetuated by romantic fools.

One look at his companion made it crystal clear that he must feel just the opposite. She'd experienced not measuring up to other females most of her life. That feeling fit like an old sweater. But now the comfortable and familiar felt worn out. The distant look in his eyes when they'd shaken hands had been obvious to someone who'd seen the reaction often.

Some women attracted men like flies to honey. She repelled most of them like bug spray.

She told herself that was fine with her. She was who she was, and she liked herself—dirty hands and all. It was a relief that good-looking Cole Taggert must think she was beneath him. It was a relief. Really.

Remembering the way her last position had ended reaffirmed her conviction. She needed this job, and she didn't need another son of another boss making unwanted advances toward her and causing trouble.

Somehow, though, she couldn't make herself believe it this time. This time it was different. Advances from Cole Taggert wouldn't be unwanted at all. CJ gripped the wheel even tighter. What had he done to her with one grin, one touch, one bark of laughter?

The ride to Laurel Glen passed in a haze of confused speculation. As she'd been told to do, CJ turned in at the second fork in the drive and, with a wave, Cole Taggert continued on to what she assumed was Laurel House.

The layout of the stables and practice ring was interesting. There were four stone and brick stable buildings in an X pattern with a competition size ring at the juncture. All the buildings were enclosed by a wide yard and cordoned off by fenced pastures. One structure showed the unmistakable evidence of the devastating fire that had taken place several months earlier.

Hope had told her about it and warned her that Laurel Glen's business was in a bit of a slump due to the dirty tricks and vandalism of an ex-employee who was currently in jail awaiting trial for his misdeeds. Many of the farm's clients had moved their animals or canceled riding lessons out of fear. Hope had assured CJ the clients would return and that her new job was secure. With a reputation like the one Ross Taggert had built, CJ had little doubt the claim was true.

She jumped out of her ancient pickup and looked around. Hope had told her she'd be stabling Morning in Stable Two, where the family kept their mares. CJ looked around, uncomfortable with the idea of unloading the palomino without talking to Hope or Ross, but Morning had been cooped up too long already.

The sweet-natured mare had been as cooperative as a lamb, but CJ didn't think that would last much longer. As if to underscore her thoughts, the racket of steel on steel resounded from the back of the trailer. Morning had apparently had enough of confinement.

"Can I help you, miss?" a man asked from behind her as she dropped the back of the trailer to the ground.

CJ stood straight and turned toward a tall man in a winter-white Stetson. "You could tell me where I can find Ross Taggert or Hope Carrington. I need to report in and get Morning settled. She's been holed up in this icebox for six hours thanks to two flat tires and turnpike construction."

"*I'm* Ross Taggert," the man said, narrowing his eyes a bit. "And you are?"

CJ wiped her dirt- and rust-covered hand on her jeans and reached out to shake her new boss's hand. "CJ Larson, sir. Nice to finally meet you."

The man stared at her, his mouth open in surprise. She had that effect on people. They never thought someone as small as she would be capable of working animals so much larger than herself, but she always proved them wrong. She had a God-given talent, and genes for the work she'd inherited from her grandfather. Daddy used to say Grandpa could train a cat to swim. It wasn't pride on CJ's part when she said she could do the same. It was fact.

"You're a girl," Ross Taggert finally said.

"Always have been, but, as I'm fully an adult now, I like to think of myself as a woman. In spite of my size I do a full day's work for a day's pay."

"I'm sure you do, but I'm sorry, Ms. Larson, Laurel Glen just isn't the place for you. I'm even more shorthanded than I was months ago. I just don't have the time to watch over you. I'm afraid you've wasted your time coming all this way. You can rest your horse here free of charge and use the cabin for a few days, but you just can't be Laurel Glen's trainer."

Chapter Two

CJ now knew what the expression poleaxed meant. "Excuse me? I don't understand. I have everything I own in this pickup and trailer, and I have a one-year contract."

"It was signed under false pretenses," Ross Taggert countered, his voice reasonable.

"I signed that contract in good faith. What false pretenses?"

"Your name is legally CJ?"

She sighed. "No. Legally it's Charity Jane. I've never been a Charity or a Jane. Believe me. CJ is the name I competed under. I've always used it for business because it's recognized. No one has ever complained before."

"There's a first time for everything. I'll give you a month's pay for your trouble, but that's as far as I'll go. All I knew other than your qualifications was that you were Charlie Larson. I don't want a woman working in this operation.''

"That's sex discrimination!" She was getting loud and genuinely outraged.

Ross Taggert shrugged. "You can always hire a lawyer."

CJ didn't have the money to hire a lawyer, and the shape of her pickup and trailer didn't exactly hide the fact. Besides, the last lawyer she'd hired managed to lose her family home to the bank through incompetence or thievery, she was still not one hundred percent sure which.

"Please. I need this job. I can't go trucking this mare back—" She stopped. What was she saying? This was the end of the line. "I don't have anywhere to go. Anywhere at all."

Ross Taggert looked a little pale. "It's nothing personal, Ms. Larson. I'm really sorry, but I can't have you working here."

CJ glanced at Morning. The mare was the last gift her parents gave her before their deaths. She couldn't endanger Morning because she'd trusted the wrong men—first Howard Gibbens, bankruptcy lawyer unexceptional, and Ross Taggert.

"Why are you being so unfair?" CJ demanded, her voice breaking, much to her chagrin. If he wouldn't change his unreasonable attitude, she'd have to sell Morning. Maybe even to him, the man destroying what was left of her life.

"She can sue, and she'll win," Cole said as he clapped his father on the shoulder, joining them at the back of the trailer. "Take my word for it. You won't have a leg to stand on. You specifically noted her gender as your reason for terminating her contract. Even I heard you. She'll probably call me as a witness."

Ross Taggert's expression hardened, and his back stiffened. "And you'd testify for her, wouldn't you?"

Cole took his hand off his father's shoulder as if he physically felt the cool tone in Ross Taggert's voice. Cole shrugged then dropped his shoulder negligently against the trailer. Then he shot her a grin that turned her knees to jelly even in the middle of her life-and-death battle. She could do little more than stare at his handsome face as he argued for her.

"I wouldn't have a choice, Dad. I'm a law-abiding citizen. I'd have to answer a subpoena. Come on. She looks every bit as capable as Hope. Hope wouldn't have hired CJ otherwise. Jeff even recommended her. CJ probably has bigger muscles than both of us. She'll do fine."

Ross Taggert shook his head, turned and walked away. He got as far as the bed of her pickup when he stopped and leaned his forearms on the side rails. He looked like a man carrying the weight of the world on his shoulders. Then he shook his head again and walked back to them.

"You know how hard having Hope working with the animals was for me. I'm not sure—I... I can't do it again."

"Can't means won't. Isn't that what Granny always said?"

The look Cole shot his father was blatant challenge and mockery at once. She couldn't imagine talking to either of her parents like that, especially in front of a stranger, but she'd never been subjected to the kind of icy tone Ross had used on Cole, either.

"Come on, Dad. Give her a chance. She looks like a nice kid. Your problems aren't her fault."

Mr. Taggert studied his son for a long moment then he raised an eyebrow. It was clear he was challenging his son right back. "All right, suppose I give you a trial, Ms. Larson. Two months. If you foul up or get hurt in any way, you're out of here. No arguments. No lawyers. If things run smoothly and I like what I see happening, then we'll talk about you staying on."

CJ looked from Ross Taggert to Cole then quickly to the father again. What had just happened? Why had he changed his mind? Since father and son seemed to have a strangely adversarial relationship, it couldn't be that he'd done it as a favor to Cole.

Cole's voice broke into her thoughts. "Tell him you accept before he goes back on his word—again."

"I accept," CJ parroted, too confused and unsettled by yo-yoing emotions to think clearly. It was going to be all right. Somehow, for some reason, Cole had talked his father into honoring her contract—at least the first two months of it. She just wished she knew why Cole had helped and why Ross Taggert had folded.

"Help her get her animal settled then show her where the cottage is," Ross ordered. "I'm supposed to go into the city with Amelia. Oh, and son, the lady considers herself a woman not a kid. You'd do well to remember that."

Cole frowned, confusion written on his handsome features. "I'll make sure she's all tucked in safe and sound," he said to his father's back, since Ross Taggert was already stalking away.

"What was that all about?" CJ asked Cole. "Why did he change his mind and why did you help me when I got the distinct impression you don't approve of me?"

Cole looked shocked. "Not so." Then he grinned—a mischievous one this time. Unfortunately, it had the same heart-tripping affect on CJ as the earlier cocky one did. "Besides," he continued, "even if that were true, I'd still have taken up your cause. I just can't help it. He says black, I say white. And I can't resist trying to get the better of him, either."

"That's terrible. You're lucky to have a father. And I don't like being used," she added, annoyed that he hadn't really been trying to help her.

Cole grinned again, unrepentant. "Don't complain. In case you didn't notice, you won this round. Now let's get this little lady unloaded and settled in her new home. I want to get a good look at her," he said as he scaled the ramp and spoke softly to Morning. His voice was mesmerizing, and by the time he was finished with Morning it was clear he had another Larson woman under the spell of his deep, soothing voice and killer grin.

Cole hoisted a box to his shoulder then maneuvered another one off the tailgate and under his arm, trapping it against his hip. CJ hadn't been kidding when she said she had everything she owned in her truck. And most of it looked like junk, if the old lamps and bric-a-brac he was carting into the cottage were any indication.

"Where do you want these?" he called to CJ as he pried open the storm door with his toe and entered the cottage's small parlor.

"On the coffee table should be fine," she said. She'd been unpacking boxes in the kitchen and the dining area behind the parlor. The cottage's only bedroom took up the space to the right of the front door. The bath was opposite the kitchen down a hall formed by the kitchen and bedroom walls.

Cole noticed that the fire he'd started gave the room a cheery glow. He unloaded his burden and stopped, staring at the book on top of the box he'd had on his shoulder.

But then CJ said, "You look like you could use this," and walked toward him, two glasses in her hands. "I had some tea left in my thermos from the trip, and there was some ice in the freezer. You probably should have taken off a layer before hauling all my stuff in.'' She smiled at him again and held out a glass.

It was an automatic response when he reached to take it and gulped down half of it in seconds. When he looked at her again, she was staring at him, her eyes huge in her delicate face. If his father saw her at that moment, he'd run screaming. She looked about twelve and not only innocent but infinitely vulnerable, too. With her coat off she was even more delicate than her height and the strength of her hands had indicated.

Cole felt such an urge to wrap his arms around her and protect her that his heart tripped. He felt things in her presence that were new and, frankly, it worried him. He should never have interfered when his father offered her a month's pay. She might be gone by now if he'd just kept his big mouth shut!

He realized that they were staring at each other and cast about for something to break the odd hold she seemed to have over him. His eyes fell once again on the Bible tossed on top of the other items in the box. It didn't look like one of those big ones people keep only to record births, deaths and marriages. Nor was it old-fashioned enough to be a family heirloom.

Nope.

It was modern but well-worn. He'd bet a month's profits that it was hers. Well, that sure broke the spell. There was nothing guaranteed to put him off like religion. He picked it up and flipped it open.

Yep.

It was hers, all right. Another Bible-thumper! He was surrounded by them!

"I should have known," he muttered as he tossed it back where he'd gotten it. Something occurred to him then, annoying him even more. His father probably saw it when he'd walked away and looked into the truck. She'd used clear plastic to tie her belongings down. Had that been his reason for not sending her on her way? Was Ross hoping she would have some influence on his wayward son?

"You should have known what?" CJ asked, frowning and looking toward her discarded holy book.

"That you're part of the church crowd like everybody else around here. That my father probably saw this and that's why he changed his mind about letting you stay. He probably thinks you'll fall in love with me and help save my lost soul the way he thinks Amelia did for him and Hope did with Jeff."

CJ's eyes widened.

"Let me save you a lot of trouble." He went on before she could react further. "It's not going to happen on this end. I don't *do* love. Got it? And, anyway, why don't all you Christians grow up and stop leaning on God like He's this big protective parent? I don't want you preaching when I'm around. Got it?"

CJ's dark eyes widened then shot sparks. "Of all the— You are a conceited moron, Cole Taggert. As if I'd fall in love with an arrogant, egotistical, self-absorbed creep like you. I don't preach. I don't force my Lord down anyone's throat. But if I meet someone who's troubled and there's wisdom in that Bible that will help, then I'll talk about God all I want. It's a free country. So far, we still have freedom to talk about our religious beliefs to others.''

"Oh, yeah? Well, since it's a free country, I don't have to listen!''

"No, you don't. It's your prerogative to go on being miserable, but let me tell you something. I've found the ones who yell the loudest about not needing God or run the fastest from His saving grace are the ones who need Him most.''

Cole gave her a cold-eyed stare. He held it just long enough to prove he wasn't running from God or her, then he turned and stormed out. He got halfway across the compound before he noticed he still had half a glass of tea in his hand. He stamped his foot. When a couple of the men working nearby snickered, he realized he'd not only sounded like a twelve-year-old with CJ, now he looked like one, too!

And he'd told *her* to grow up?

The woman just plain confounded him the way no other ever had. She scared Cole to death. He'd always joked that he'd run far and fast if he ever met a woman like CJ. And now it had happened.

And he couldn't run.

He had to stay at Laurel Glen. He knew being there held the key to the rest of his life. He and Ross had to face the past together before Cole could move on, but he just couldn't seem to confront his father openly. There was something fragile about Ross, ever since they'd solved the mystery of who was trying to destroy Laurel Glen.

Even Ross's current happiness with Amelia and his odd fascination with church hadn't changed it. Ross still didn't look a day over forty, and he hadn't slowed down in any way. He was the picture of middle-aged good health, but he seemed breakable to Cole. Cole admitted that he didn't know his father well, but he'd always felt a connection to him, and something wasn't right.

Cole turned toward the house. It wouldn't hurt to see if Ross and Amelia had left for their appointment. Cole wondered if his father had seemed okay to Aunt Meg. And maybe Hope would be there. Then he could bend her ear a little for putting CJ Larson in such a tight spot. He wouldn't mention how much of a spot CJ's presence put him in, though. No. Hope was too perceptive for him to chance exposing that much of his feelings.

CJ stormed across the little parlor and slammed the door behind Cole Taggert.

"Of all the unmitigated nerve!" she growled and stormed toward the kitchen.

She smacked her glass of iced tea down, then groaned when it sloshed all over her and the counter. She just couldn't get her mind around his attitude. The way he'd spoken you'd think Christians hid horns and a pointed tail. Why would someone turn on God the way Cole had instead of turning *to* Him?

That gave CJ pause and, as always, whenever she let her temper get the better of her, any pause gave her enough time to recognize that she'd slipped into bad habits. The biggest problem in her spiritual life was her temper.

She looked out the window above the sink and could almost hear her grandfather's admonishing words. *What would kindness have shown him about the Lord? You don't win Him souls by shouting at people.*

Ashamed of her lack of control, CJ thought back to the question that had started her thinking more calmly. Why was Cole so defensive about faith?

A knock at the back door drew her attention. She opened it expecting that Cole had returned with the glass and an apology. But it was a woman about her own height with chin-length dark hair.

"CJ? Hi. I'm Hope Carrington. I'm so sorry my father reacted badly to your arrival. I really didn't think he'd refuse to honor your contract."

"Come in. My house is your house, at least for two months. I take it you never told your father that his new trainer was a woman."

"No. I'd counted on being here when you arrived. Honestly! He's gotten worse instead of better. Thank goodness Cole stepped in. Don't worry about the two-month trial. You'll knock his socks off. I'll talk to him and calm him down, too. And speaking of knocking someone's socks off, what did you do to my brother?"

CJ shrugged. "For some reason he didn't like finding out I'm a Christian. He told me not to talk about God in his hearing. Would you like some tea or hot cocoa?''

"Cocoa would be perfect," Hope said and sat at the little kitchen table.

CJ looked at her half-empty glass. "I've been here less than two hours and I've had arguments with both the men who live here. Mind telling me what I'm doing wrong? It really looks like a beautiful operation, and I'd like to stay."

"And you will. My father isn't an ogre."

"I'm sure he isn't. In fact, he seemed genuinely upset to be sending me on my way, but he was just as determined that I leave. It really didn't make much sense."

"My mother was killed by a horse. My father had to put him down to get him to stop trampling her. And early last summer when Harry Donovan was playing all his dirty tricks, I was hurt by some falling hay bales. Then, in September, Donovan tampered with Dad's new wife's SUV. If Dad hadn't figured out how to stop her car, she'd probably have been killed. He was always overprotective, but since that day he's been unbearable. And you don't even want to know how bad he's been since I got pregnant. He's a basket case."

"Is your father a man of faith? Something Cole said made me think he was." Of course, she'd never repeat what else he'd said.

"He is now. He tried to handle everything life threw at him for years alone, but when Laurel Glen was so threatened, Amelia got him to turn to the Lord. He's just a little slow to hand over every worry. Bad habits die hard.''

"Tell me about it. I wasn't exactly sweet-tempered with your brother. I hope this doesn't sound like prying but why does Cole hate God so much? His reaction to seeing my Bible was more than a little over the top.''

"I don't know. Not really,'' Hope said, her eyes narrowed a bit. "He blames Mom's death on God, but I don't know why. I only know I never would have gotten through her death without my faith.''

"It was the same for me when my parents were killed and after Grandpa died last year. I couldn't have endured those losses on my own strength.''

"Cole was angry with God from the day of our mother's death, but he didn't go to church even back then. It was bound to be harder for Cole than me, of course, but I always thought his burden would have been easier to bear if he'd turned to the Lord.''

"Why would it be harder for him?''

"Dad bought the horse that killed Mom for Cole's fifteenth birthday. When it threw Cole, my brother was convinced the horse was dangerous. Dad wanted him to get back on and ride. Mom intervened and rode him instead. She was killed, and Cole saw the whole thing.''

CJ's heart went out to the confused adolescent boy Cole must have been. But she was just as curious about why he was bitter against God when he hadn't been a churchgoer before that. "Maybe he needed a target for his anger," she speculated.

"Oh, he had one right here at Laurel Glen! My father. Their relationship has never been the same."

"I noticed they have sort of a strained relationship. At least on Cole's side. Your poor father."

"Cole isn't trying to be cruel, believe me. He hasn't been any easier on himself. He blamed himself, too. You wouldn't believe how self-destructive he was that year after her death. He finally went too far when he stole a police car and went riding around the back roads with the lights and sirens on. You'll probably hear that Cole was sent away to military school by order of the court. That was why. It straightened him out, but he stayed away until last year."

"But he was only a kid."

"A determined one. Dad should probably have forced him to come home when he was allowed. They might have gotten back on track but in the long run it was just as well. One of the things Harry Donovan was trying to do last summer was frame Cole. And it almost worked. Back then with his attitude and juvenile record, Cole wouldn't have stood a chance."

"The Lord really does work in mysterious ways, doesn't He? It's uncanny how He can take what is clearly a mistake and use it for the good. I'm still waiting to find out how He's going to use a crooked bankruptcy lawyer for the good."

Hope smiled. "You're here, aren't you? Remem-

ber the old saying, 'Today is the first day of the rest
of your life.' Your life is about to change, CJ. I just
know it.''

CJ was sure it was. She just wasn't sure it would
be a change for the better.

Chapter Three

Cole stopped dead in his tracks just inside the doorway of Laurel House's formal parlor. It was a voice—new but familiar—that froze him in place. It was a voice he feared would begin haunting his dreams that very night. It belonged to CJ Larson.

"So then I have you to thank for my chewed up ball cap, Mrs. Taggert?" CJ said, causing a round of laughter.

"Please, CJ, it's Amelia. And, CJ, don't believe a word he says. If Ross had warned me that I shouldn't hide treats in my pockets, Queen Morgana wouldn't have gone looking for them and found my Phillies cap."

"Now it's *my* fault?" his father asked with mock outrage. All his father did was smile around Amelia.

Cole stared at the group. Hope and Jeff sat close together on one of the sofas that flanked the fireplace, and Amelia and his father sat opposite on its twin.

They, as well as Aunt Meg, who occupied a chair near the roaring fire, were all dressed for dinner per Laurel House tradition. CJ sat across from Aunt Meg, leaving the chair nearest Cole empty. That one completed a cozy horseshoe about the fireplace.

CJ, he noted, was dressed all wrong. Sure she'd changed, but she still wore jeans that were clearly for work, as was her plaid flannel shirt. Didn't the woman own anything but work clothes? And what did she think dress for dinner meant? He was sure she'd been told.

Dressing for dinner was a hard-and-fast Laurel House rule set up by Granny Taggert before Cole's grandfather was born. If any family member had ever shown up dressed in work clothes the way CJ was, they'd have been banished to the kitchen for a week.

He frowned. Her attire wasn't really the point here, though, was it? Amelia had told him not to bring Elizabeth because this was supposed to be a family gathering. So what was CJ doing here laughing with his family before dinner? CJ Larson was *not* family. And she never would be—not if he had a say in it!

This was starting to smack more and more of matchmaking on his sister's part. And maybe now she'd enlisted his father and Amelia. What had Hope been planning to do when CJ arrived? Present her as the perfect person to save the wayward son and drag him kicking and screaming into the fold? After all, when he and Ross had gotten into an argument over Amelia, hadn't she forced his father to accompany her to church to make up for the things he'd said?

"Cole, I'd begun to think you'd deserted us again tonight," he heard Aunt Meg say.

Cole blinked and focused his attention on her. "Sorry, sweetheart, Thad Burton tried to take a jump Galaxy wasn't ready for."

"That boy is going to drive André and Courtney Burton into a rest home," Aunt Meg declared, laughter in her tone. "How is the poor horse?"

Cole couldn't help chuckling in spite of his annoyance at finding CJ there. "Well, Galaxy's going to be fine. Thad, however, was grounded for life, last I heard."

"I'll try talking to the kid again. He just keeps trying to push the envelope too far," Ross said. "You are staying for dinner, aren't you, son?"

Cole glanced at CJ, who was studiously ignoring him in favor of the beverage in her hand. If she was uncomfortable with his presence, so be it. This was his family. And he was staying. "Of course, I'm staying. Amelia commanded me to show up, and I'm here. Dressed in my Sunday best for dinner like a good boy. Wouldn't want to get sent to my room. Again."

His father let out a bark of laughter, and Amelia crossed her arms, glaring at both of them. Cole got the idea that the glare she sent his way was really over his pointed remark about dressing for dinner and not over an incident that had become a family joke.

"Cole was a bad boy, and Amelia sent him to his room," Hope explained for CJ's benefit. "He's *fre-*

quently a bad boy," his sister added through gritted teeth.

So Hope hadn't missed his dig at CJ, either. Neither had Jeff, if his have-you-lost-your-mind expression was anything to go by. Only CJ and his father had not caught his meaning. He felt small and didn't like it, but he didn't like feeling trapped, either.

"I thought you and Mr. Taggert just met last August?" CJ asked, even more confused with Hope's explanation but still blissfully unaware she had broken a long-standing Laurel House rule.

"We did," Amelia replied. "Cole was twenty-nine at the time. And he deserved it. We like to think he's matured since celebrating his thirtieth birthday last month."

"Speaking of birthdays," Ross said, clearing his throat. "Amie and I wanted you all here because we have an announcement about a birthday and we wanted to celebrate," he continued as he settled his arm around Amelia. "A new member of the Taggert family is scheduled to arrive in the end of August."

"No, Dad, I'm due in September," Hope protested. "Though I appreciate you trying to cut a few weeks off the time. Besides, what's with the announcement? Everyone knows about the baby already."

Ross beamed at Hope. "Not your baby, princess. Ours. Amie's pregnant and due the last week of August."

"What! Why haven't you said anything before now?" Aunt Meg demanded.

"Because I'm irregular, and for a while I didn't realize it. Then," she added with a pause and a wry glance at Ross, "because Ross has been a bit worried how y'all would react to the news. But when I couldn't zip even my most generous slacks this morning, I decided we'd waited long enough."

Amid protest from everyone that a baby was always joyous news, Cole sank into the lone empty chair. A baby. He was all up for the uncle scene, but a brother or sister? He'd considered the possibility in the abstract, of course. Amelia would make a great mother, and his father was still a young man. Back in September, when Ross tanked his relationship with Amelia, thinking he was too old for marriage and fatherhood, it had been Cole himself who'd sent his father scrambling after her. But now that a baby was a fact, it was a little tough to get his brain to wrap itself around the idea.

"Cole, you haven't said anything," Ross said, dragging Cole out of his thoughts as a round of hugs ended and everyone sat back down.

Casting about for some comment that wouldn't widen the gulf between him and his father, Cole thought back to his own childhood with this man and smiled. "Do I have to wait till the kid can walk before I can put him on Cobby?"

He breathed a silent sigh of relief when Ross threw back his head and laughed. "No, but I don't think old Cobby will appreciate it if you climb aboard to hold him in front of you the way you helped give Hope her first ride," his father joked.

"And what if *she* is afraid of horses?" Amelia demanded.

"*He* might be a *she,* but this baby will be a Taggert. No way will a Taggert be afraid of horses," Ross said, then added, "she'll probably be as fearless as her mother. Oh-oh." He groaned comically. "I think I feel gray threading its way through my hair already. I still haven't gotten over the shock of the first time I saw you up in a tree getting that perfect shot of Laurel House."

Cole snickered. "And Hope's providing a partner in crime. Good luck, you four. It's going to be interesting around here for the next several years. I think I'll play the part of adoring brother and uncle. I'll just sit back and indulge the little ones while you guys clean up the messes and untangle the disasters."

Ross groaned again. "Another generation of double trouble." He looked at Jeff then Cole. "I'll never forget that first time you two disappeared for hours. Jeff was about seven, and Cole was five. We were all frantic. I found them on the south boundary of Laurel Glen, Cobby tied to a bush and those two skinny-dipping in the creek. Problem was, we were in a drought, and the creek was nearly dried up. It looked more like they were taking a mud bath."

Jeff laughed. "The look on your face is something I'll never forget. Especially when Cole told you we weren't lost. We knew exactly where we were."

The story set the tone for the rest of the evening

as everyone traded stories from their childhood. Everyone but CJ.

Several hours later, Cole pulled his collar up around his neck and made his way to the stables. He stopped to check on Mischief, his gelding, then moved on to Cobby, the old Welsh cob pony he'd spoken of. "Hey, old boy," he murmured as he smoothed his hand along the thirty-three-year-old pony's back. "It looks like you'll have a new master soon. But you'll always be my first love. You know that, don't you?" The pony whuffled and tossed his head as if in answer.

Cole laughed, but a noise in the yard drew his attention. Frowning, still suspicious of anything out of the ordinary after last summer's traumatic events, he left Cobby and followed the sound. He wasn't really surprised when he found CJ petting Morning and talking to the mare through the yard door to her stall in Stable Two.

"Oh, hello," she called when he got near. "You're out here sort of late. You don't have to worry. I already did a last check of all the animals."

"I'm not a bit worried," he told her. "I wouldn't have pushed my father to honor your contract if I had the slightest doubt about your abilities. I was actually visiting an old pal."

She glanced toward the stable he'd just left. "The Welsh cob?"

"Cobby was my first horse. Hope rode him, too, but he's always been mine."

"And now your little brother or sister will ride him."

Cole shook his head. "That sounds so strange. It's always been just Hope and me." He wasn't jealous. Just unused to the idea.

"You'll have a ball spoiling both babies. Is Hope helping find Laurel Glen a foreman the way she did a trainer?"

"If she was before you showed up, she won't be now. I imagine Dad will continue his search alone. Why? Do you have a sorority sister looking for a job?" he teased.

CJ shook her head and laughed. It was a free, clear-as-a-bell sound that made Cole's heart swell.

"I don't have sorority sisters. I didn't go to any college except the one of hard knocks. My parents were killed when I was in the end of my senior year of high school. I turned down my scholarship to stay home with Grandpa. When he died, the business fell apart."

"It was his farm?" Cole asked.

"And his father's before him. It was going really well. My parents were on a trip out west looking at a stud when their small plane crashed. Grandpa and I kept the operation going, but when he died it was all over but the auction. We kept the wolf at bay for seven years, but with Grandpa gone—" She shook her head and shrugged.

Cole frowned. "So now you have no family and you're all but homeless. It doesn't seem fair." He wanted to hug her and offer comfort. His heart felt tight and longed for some unnamed something from CJ that he couldn't identify.

"Grandpa always said fair was a weather forecast. I try to look at what God's given me instead of looking at what He hasn't. It works most of the time. When it doesn't, I ask for the strength to endure. They say He never closes a door without opening a window. I like to think Laurel Glen is that window."

Cole rolled his eyes. *Here comes a sermon,* he thought, but after a moment of silence, he glanced at CJ. She just continued to stroke Morning's golden muzzle.

"Earlier today you said believers are childish because we rely on God." She spoke just above a whisper. "I know you were trying to insult me, but you missed by a mile. What you don't understand is that being childlike is what He demands of us. He wants us to rely on Him as our heavenly Father the same way we relied on our earthly fathers as children. That kind of faith gives even adults security in times of trouble. We know that nothing eternally bad can happen to us because He's watching over us. Do you remember that time in your life when your father was the be-all and end-all of safety and you basked in the light of his approval?"

At that moment CJ didn't look particularly strong, but neither did she look childish with the moonlight shimmering in her hair and painting her face silver with its ethereal rays. She patted the mare and turned a sad smile on him. She looked infinitely desirable and she radiated a compelling kind of goodness that had him frowning in consternation. He was the family bad boy who purported to find virtue repellant. Instead, in her, it drew him like a moth to flame.

"He was a great father when I was a kid," Cole said, determined to resist getting burned.

"I gathered that from the talk tonight. And if you're worried, I doubt Ross realized how much news of the new baby disconcerted you. You did a good job covering up." Her voice drifted into the night as if it came from a heavenly being, and a shiver went through him.

Then CJ covered a yawn. "Oh, I better hit the hay. Six o'clock comes along whether you're ready for it or not. Good night." She turned but pivoted. "Morning's a good listener, Cole. And she never preaches. Close her up for the night when you're done." She smiled sagely and walked toward her cabin.

Cole stared after her—a little bit of a thing who had read his emotions across a room and who stirred him as no other woman ever had. "That is one scary lady you have there, Morning," he told the palomino. "You don't seem bothered," he said, contemplating the mare's placid stance. "But I'll tell you something. She scares me to death."

Chapter Four

CJ put the curry comb in the cupboard, then patted Morning. "See you tomorrow, girl," she said. The mare whuffled an enthusiastic response, making CJ chuckle. After a few more loving strokes to Morning's velvety muzzle, CJ headed toward the exit. At the first stall in the next stable building, she stopped and watched the gelding called Mischief with a troubled heart, wondering if she were about to be fired because of him.

She'd been told the story of how Cole had rescued the Arabian mix from an abusive owner. He was a beautiful animal with a dark sable coat and a mane and tail that were a surprising golden white. Her heart had been warmed by the tale and the way Cole had championed the animal while seeing that the owner was punished for his abuse of more than one of his horses. But now she was just plain angry with Cole.

He'd apparently lost all interest in the animal. Because of Mischief's high-strung nature, one of the men was at the hospital getting his broken arm set. Her trial could be over.

She sighed and stretched her back. She'd just put in three very full days and she was bone tired. Maybe even a little short-tempered and pessimistic. Since she'd arrived she had worked with Hope, who'd taken on the job of getting CJ oriented at Laurel Glen. She'd come to believe she would fit into the routine at the farm just fine.

But even so, after only three days, CJ recognized a problem when she was faced with one. Mischief wasn't responding to Hope's training methods, and CJ felt more definite action had to be taken. The animal was a problem with a capital P. And to make matters worse, Cole hadn't been around, and he really needed to be there, showing the gelding not only who was boss but that Cole could be trusted to keep him safe and secure.

CJ patted Mischief and turned away, prepared to go to battle for her job. If she won the first skirmish, she'd forge ahead for the sweet-natured gelding's sake. With a great deal of annoyance and anxiety over the coming confrontation with Ross Taggert and his mercurial son, CJ headed toward Laurel House.

Halfway up the hill, her anxiety changed course. If she didn't get fired and Cole agreed to cooperate where Mischief was concerned, he would be around a lot more. He with his beautiful eyes and wide, smiling mouth. His charm and quicksilver wit. And he would look right through her to his beautiful companion Elizabeth.

She almost changed direction, but there was no use putting off the inevitable. Besides, there was Mischief's well-being to consider. Feeling utterly selfish for her momentary cowardice, she pushed on and crested the hill by the garages. As she crossed the stone terrace, CJ heard soft laughter coming from the back of the house.

"Hello," she called as she approached the corner of the stone mansion.

"CJ?" she heard Meg Taggert call in response. "We're back here. Come around."

It was as CJ rounded the terrace that she realized her heightened state was not due to worry but to a strange sort of excitement she could only define as longing. There was no denying it, her heart was pounding in anticipation of seeing and being close to Cole again. She'd missed him.

To her disappointment, when she drew closer to the group, Cole wasn't among the family members roasting marshmallows in front of a charming outdoor fireplace.

Ross Taggert smiled. "Pull up a chair and join us. I found out Amie never had smores. Can you imagine such a neglected education?" he said as he put a square of world-famous Pennsylvania milk chocolate on a graham cracker. Next, he added a steaming toasted marshmallow before pressing the concoction between the crackers.

"There you go, sweetheart." Ross handed Amelia

the dessert then he licked his fingers as his eyes sparkled with a joy so pure it made CJ's heart ache. From that moment on, she thought, she'd have a hard time thinking of Ross Taggert as anything more threatening than a tall, lean teddy bear.

CJ felt a wry smile tip her lips. She was wise enough not to share her mental image with her new boss. "I can see it would be tough to resist correcting such a shameful lacking as soon as possible. But isn't it a little chilly for a sing-along by the fire?"

"Not with warm clothes and hot spiced cider. Seriously. It's really nice close in near the fire. Come join us," Ross all but ordered. He jumped up to pull a padded patio chair into the semicircle as Meg and Amelia shifted to accommodate her arrival.

"I didn't mean to intrude," CJ told them as she sat where bidden.

"You're not intruding," Meg assured her.

She grimaced nervously. "Still."

"I told you the other night when I invited you for dinner—we're all family at Laurel Glen," Amelia told her.

"You look a little worried. Is there something wrong?" Ross asked.

"We had a problem with Mischief."

"I'm trying to monitor him but I don't always have as much time as I'd like. He hasn't gotten aggressive with you, has he?"

She shook her head. "But he's still afraid to be tied, and it caused a problem about an hour ago. I hate to tell you this, but Raymond is in the ER having his arm set.''

Ross's gaze sharpened, and her teddy bear image of him disappeared. It was just wishful thinking, she told herself, as she waited for him to tell her to pack up and move on.

"From now on, if there's a problem with one of the men or animals, I want to be told immediately."

CJ let out the breath she'd been holding. "Normally, I would have, but Mischief needed attention, too. He'd kicked clear through the wall of his stall and had a six-inch splinter in his knee."

Ross nodded. "Fine. The men aren't your problem. You're here as a trainer not as a foreman. I don't want to overburden you." He sighed, and his shoulders slumped. "I don't know how I'm going to tell Cole he has to get rid of Mischief. He loves that gelding, but I was always afraid he wouldn't work out."

CJ hadn't wanted this! She didn't want to keep her job and wind up losing Mischief for Cole, even if he didn't care as much as everyone seemed to think about the gelding.

"But he wasn't trying to hurt anyone," CJ protested. "I planned to have Raymond brush him as a distraction while I worked on the knee. But then Georgie tried to tie him so he could give me a hand just as Ray dropped the curry brush. Mischief shied back and stepped on Ray's arm as he bent to pick up the brush. In no way did Mischief *try* to hurt anyone.''

Ross blew a relieved breath through his pursed lips. "Then it was definitely an accident?"

Relieved, too, CJ nodded. All she had to do was convince him of a need to change the gelding's training program. "Accidental though it was, Mr. Taggert, it did happen, and it could have been prevented. I know Mischief's behavior is because of the way he was mistreated before Cole rescued him, but I still feel that horse needs a much more intensive and deliberate program. Other than his fear of being tied, he's obviously still kicking and weaving in his stall. I know Hope wanted to go easy with him, but now he's hurt himself and one of the men."

"Let's give your training techniques a try. I'd like to see what you can do with a problem, and I sure can't imagine him getting worse. I really prefer not to have that conversation with Cole."

CJ couldn't hold her tongue. "It would help if Mischief were to see more of him. Everyone says he cares so much about that horse, but he hasn't been near him since I arrived."

Ross frowned. "I'm sorry, CJ. I guess Hope forgot to mention that Cole left to settle some affairs in California. He had no idea how long he'd be gone. What with his half of the practice to sell, a condo to off-load and financial matters to resolve and transfer, there's no telling how long he'll be out there. It could be a couple of months, but believe me, he normally spends a good deal of time with Mischief. The trouble is Mischief's bad habits are mostly linked to stall and care. He behaves when Cole rides him."

CJ fought to hide her disappointment that Cole was gone. And what bothered her was that the disappointment was for herself—not Mischief. It didn't matter that he'd left for the west coast, she tried to tell herself. It didn't matter that he'd left without saying goodbye. And it certainly didn't matter that she'd more than likely be gone when he returned. Or that he'd probably planned it that way. It didn't matter. It couldn't.

Cole sighed. He was almost home.

Home.

He smiled as his big SUV ate up the last miles between him and Laurel Glen. He looked out over the bright green landscape of Chester County and put the windows down, letting the early June air stream in. He took a deep breath.

Home.

For the first time since he was sixteen, he thought of Laurel Glen as home. While he'd been in California, the feeling had grown until palm trees, smog and in-line skaters had come to feel as if born of an alien world.

He felt foolish to have run from this place because an ill-mannered slip of a woman had invaded his territory with her sweet face and knowing smiles. There was no rhyme or reason to his feelings, so he'd discounted them and chalked them up to underused, leftover hormones. He'd certainly curtailed his nighttime activities since moving back to Pennsylvania.

At long last, he passed Lavender Hill, where his

sister, Hope, and her husband, Jeff, lived. They'd opened a training camp that combined equestrian riding and competition with private schooling at a nearby institution. Within the first several months of opening their doors they had a full house. Jeff's reputation in the equine world was that good.

Laurel Glen had benefited because they had taken some overflow animals. Unfortunately, Cole's absence had made a good situation for his family not so good. They'd needed him, but problems with the sale of both the practice and the condo had held him in California longer than the two months he'd anticipated. The upside was that other than waking in the night with a strange longing in his heart and an image of CJ imprinted in his mind, he could hardly remember what she looked like.

Cole shook his head and chuckled. "Yeah, right, Taggert." Who was he trying to kid? He hadn't forgotten a thing about CJ Larson. Not her golden hair. Not her bright smile. Not her huge, brown eyes. And certainly not all the unruly, unexpected emotions she dragged out of him.

As Cole turned into Laurel Glen's long drive and drove under its iron arch, his heart constricted. He was thankful he hadn't missed this time of the year. The laurel lining the drive was just coming into bloom, and its white and pink flowers brightened an already vibrant day.

It was a picture-perfect scene that was, for a vet or livestock owner, an attractive nuisance on the best of days and a nightmare on the worst. True, it was an area of the property that had been doubly fenced off, and it was the most carefully patrolled section of fencing on the farm. But it was still the craziest thing he'd ever seen, and he'd grown up with it.

Cole grinned. Unless someone knew Granny Taggert they would never understand what had possessed his great-grandfather to allow even one of the poisonous plants on the property, let alone the hundreds of them Granny had insisted should line the drive. Granny had loved laurel, and that was the only answer anyone who knew her had ever needed.

He was sure Amelia had already shot several rolls of film of the scene from every conceivable angle. His lips curved in a helpless smile. Unless, of course, his father had wrapped her in cotton by now. The smile grew as he imagined the argument that would have ensued if Ross attempted to coddle his delicate-looking wife.

The stables and barn came into view as he crested the hill. They were rebuilding Stable Four. Finances must be looking up more than he'd thought.

The last laugh is on you, Harry Donovan. You didn't destroy Laurel Glen, after all.

And that knowledge lifted a huge burden of guilt off Cole's shoulders. He hadn't wanted to leave Ross and Hope alone to handle what had looked like a collapsing business, but distance was something he'd needed.

Cole's wandering thoughts left him unprepared for the sight of CJ cautiously approaching a prancing black monster that could have been a twin to the horse that killed his mother. He was out of the SUV and between trainer and stallion before he remembered setting the brake.

"What do you think you're doing?" CJ asked from behind him. The horse looked as perplexed to find Cole there as Cole was to be there. What *was* he doing? Besides making a fool of himself, that is.

Mindful of the two thousand pounds of confused dynamite in front of him, Cole slowly turned ninety degrees so he could look at CJ and keep a watchful eye on the horse—a horse he was grateful to for the distraction he provided. It gave him something to think about other than the answer to her perfectly reasonable question.

Someone had once said the best defense is a good offense. "Better question," Cole countered. "What do you think *you're* doing?"

"My job. Your turn," she snapped.

"I was, uh, keeping you from getting hurt?"

"If I want your help or anyone else's, I'll ask for it."

"Would you? You aren't supposed to be working any green animals alone. If my father saw this, you'd be out on your ear. I wonder what would happen if I told him what I saw down here."

"Absolutely nothing. Demon isn't all that green."

"He is from what I can see."

"I'm no fool. I've been training horses practically since the day I learned to walk. In fact, I started learning how to work with one before I learned to ride. Now if you'll excuse me, I have an animal to put away. The training session appears to be over, thanks to you.'' She pushed by him.

Cole felt his face heat. He said nothing else. No sooner had she passed him than she began to croon to the black beast, her voice sweet and gentle. Cole closed his eyes, listening for a few foolish seconds to the voice that had haunted his sleepless nights. The truth was he'd give anything if she'd talk to him that way.

Disgusted, Cole climbed into the SUV and headed up the hill toward Laurel House. He'd hoped CJ would be gone when he returned from California and, conversely, he'd feared she would be. And now he remembered why. It looked as if his trip and attempt at distance had been nothing but a great big waste of time.

Chapter Five

"Hey, there, big boy. Don't you worry. The big mean grump will be gone soon," CJ crooned, hinting that Cole had better move along. He was such a distraction. It had taken him all of ten seconds to irritate her beyond reason. What was it about him?

CJ carefully approached the big black, trying to soothe him while putting Cole out of her thoughts. But she couldn't because, though she hated to admit it, Cole had been right. Demon was green, skittish and not ready to be trusted. An audience only seemed to make him worse. Once he calmed down, she'd take him to his stall for a rubdown. Any chance she'd had of reaching the yearling today was gone. Not because Cole had upset Demon, but because Cole's sudden appearance had unnerved her, and that nervousness would transmit itself to the animal.

She wished someone had told her he would be arriving home today, but it wasn't really any of her business. She couldn't expect her new friend Hope to warn her about Cole's arrival when CJ had denied any interest in him. As far as Hope knew, there was nothing but irritation between her brother and Laurel Glen's new trainer. CJ intended to keep it that way. She only wished it were true.

Well, it probably *was* true on Cole's part. CJ doubted he'd thought of her even once during the time he'd been gone. And she wasn't fool enough to think he'd rushed into that ring for any reason other than that, according to Hope, Demon was a near duplicate to the horse who had killed their mother. It had been nothing but a knee-jerk reaction on his part.

"CJ, was that Cole I saw drive in a while ago?" Ross Taggert called up the aisle as she left Demon's stall an hour later.

"Yes, sir, it was. I guess I should warn you, we had a little altercation."

"Oh?"

"He thought Demon was dangerous and rushed into the ring. I don't suppose I took his interference all too well. I was working Demon alone. I know you want someone around when I have him in the ring, but no one except that new stable hand was around. Demon doesn't take well to strangers. It seems to make him nervous. I just thought you should know we argued."

For a long moment Ross looked toward the big black who stood quietly in his stall munching on his feed. Ross pursed his lips a little and nodded. "I appreciate your honesty, CJ. Let's try for a compromise. If no one Demon is used to is available, have someone watch from Stable Three. He can keep an eye on you through the window in the step-in door. As for any words you had with Cole, they're your business. I've had more of them than you can imagine. You don't want me for a referee, believe me.

"I imagine Demon was a shock for my son. Now that he's back, I'd like Cole to take a long, hard look at that horse for me. I'd like his opinion."

"He has wonderful form and he's not all that wild," she assured Ross. "I've worked with worse, believe me. He's just nervous around strangers."

"That's something you're going to have to work out of him, or he'll be no good to Jeff's students as a show animal. And I'm sure you've worked with tough cases, but I don't usually let an animal that skittish on the place. I only took him to keep Hope off of him while she's expecting. Still, he's gone if my son thinks he's dangerous. If I see Cole first, I'll send him down."

CJ could hardly tell her boss to keep his son away because he made *her* nervous, especially when that son was the farm's vet. So she nodded and went to her office to catch up on some paperwork. It was probably half an hour later when a tap on the door drew her attention. Somehow she knew before she looked up that it was Cole. But even prepared as she was, the sight of him still jolted her. In the bright sunlight with Demon as a distraction, she'd been able to ignore much of Cole's impact. Now, however, he was not so easy to disregard.

"Your father wanted you to take a look at Demon," she told him and looked at her ledger. "He's in the stall next to Mischief."

"From the brief glance I had of him earlier, he looks to be in pretty good health."

"He wanted your opinion of him as far as safety goes."

Cole looked haunted when she glanced up. "Oh, that kind of opinion. Amelia didn't make it clear exactly what Dad wanted. I thought he meant healthwise. It's nice to know he trusts my opinion. Shall we go have a look?"

CJ stood, resigned that Cole wasn't taking the hint. If he wasn't going to leave her in peace she might as well get everything over with all at once. "Maybe since you're here you can have a look at Mischief. He's come a long way since you've been gone."

"He's the main reason I came down. You've been working with him?"

"I felt I had to. The longer habits like his go unchecked the harder they are to break. Right now we're working on the weaving. He's almost stopped, but I haven't taken away the blocks."

"Blocks?"

"Come on, I'll show you."

CJ led the way, relieved to be out of the confining space of her office. It had never seemed quite so small before. But then Cole was apt to do that—shrink a room by his very presence.

They stopped first at Demon's stall. Cole entered calmly, any agitation he'd shown earlier gone.

"Now aren't you a beautiful boy?" The horse backed away a step or two then stopped, regarding Cole steadily. He usually shied and tried to flee strangers. "I hear someone has high hopes for you," Cole continued. "What do you say? Huh, fella? You going to win some little girl the gold someday?"

Demon canted his head first in one direction then the other as if considering the question. His bright, intelligent gaze seemed to zero in on Cole. Then he knocked his muzzle into Cole's chest and whuffled.

Cole chuckled and stroked the black's shiny coat. It was easy to see why Cole was so highly thought of in his profession. CJ had heard nothing but praise for him and his way with animals, but she hadn't seen him in action until now. Phenomenal was too bland a description.

He stayed in the stall with Demon for a good ten minutes, ignoring her and the rest of the world as the handlers moved around the building cleaning stalls, measuring feed and ushering select animals out into the bright sunlight for washing.

"He's a beautiful animal," Cole said as he stepped into the aisle. "Who owns him?"

"Jeff Carrington."

"Ah. The plot thickens. Don't tell me. Let me guess. Jeff picked up Demon for a song, and he plans to give him to just the right scholarship student when he's ready for the ring. Right?"

CJ shrugged. Since she'd arrived, she had learned the generosity of the Taggerts and Carringtons knew almost no bounds. "There's actually already a boy who'll be riding Mr. March until Demon is trained and old enough for competition. And Jeff did say he got him for a steal. You don't think that's true?''

Cole chuckled. ''Only Jeff would consider what he probably paid for this animal as anything near a steal. Jeff hasn't got a frugal bone in his body. So tell me, what is it you've done to Mischief?''

''Well, the first thing I worked on was his weaving. And here's how we cured him.''

Cole turned and walked toward the next stall where his rescued mount was housed. He stopped short, nearly walking into the half bricks she'd suspended from heavy string in the doorway. ''What on earth is this contraption?''

''My grandfather taught me this trick years ago. You hang the blocks over the stall door so they divide the space into thirds. If Mischief starts weaving while he heads out, which is when most horses exhibit the behavior, he bumps the line and starts the blocks swinging. It distracts him, and he stops the weaving.''

Cole frowned. ''What's with the straps and chains above his hocks, then? I don't like the look of that. This animal went through a pretty rough time.''

CJ tried to hold on to her temper. Did he think she was trying to be cruel? Maybe her methods would look harsh to someone who was used to coddling their animals, but Cole and Hope were raised to know better. It was clear they had over-compensated for Mischief's early life and had spoiled him.

She took a deep breath and explained. ''He was

kicking his stall so much that the wall was in splinters by the time I was here three days. When I had to pull a chunk of wood out of his leg, I spoke to Ross about more extreme measures. Mischief was going to hurt himself even worse than he already had. This way he chastises himself. The links give him a good knock on the cannon bone every time he kicks. It doesn't hurt him much, and it certainly hurts a lot less than having six-inch splinters pulled out of his knees. As you can see, the new wall is in pretty good shape, which means he's learning.''

"I guess when I left, he got agitated, but I had to get—'' He broke off what he'd been about to say and began again. "I, uh, I had some things to deal with. I'm sorry I questioned your methods. Obviously, what you're doing is working.''

She accepted his apology with a sharp nod. "I know he's special to you. He's next up to be washed down. Do you want to watch? Today I'm going to start working with his tendency to fight restraint. He has to learn to be tied or the men can't work with him, and neither can his vet.''

"I just have someone hold his harness while I work with him or while someone else grooms him. I know he looks completely undisciplined, but he's come a long way,'' Cole protested.

"That's what I hear. Not once has he pushed anyone in the mud, for instance,'' she said with a grin, alluding to an incident with Elizabeth that had prompted Cole to ask for Hope's help.

Cole chuckled. "I see little sister is still carrying tales."

CJ covered her stomach-flipping response to his chuckle by opening the stall to ready Mischief for his washing. She removed the straps and chains from his legs, then turned Mischief over to Cole so he could lead him from the stall to the snubbing post.

Cole looked at the rope looped over her shoulder. "I'm almost afraid to ask how you plan to address his fear of being tied with a rope."

"It's gonna hurt you a lot more than it does him. Believe me," she assured him. As they walked toward the place where she would work with Mischief, CJ explained what she would and wouldn't be doing.

"One thing you'll never see me do is secure him with a neck rope. A panicky horse can dislocate vertebrae too easily. In a worst-case scenario, he could choke himself or break his neck. What I do instead is make a loop around his body. I make it snug but not tight, and secure it with a bowline knot so it can't slip. Keeping the knot under his body, I'll pass the free end of the rope between his front legs then through the underside of the halter and tie it to the snubbing post. You'll see."

After giving Cole a few minutes with Mischief, CJ led the recalcitrant gelding to the post and went through the procedure she'd explained to Cole. He watched, fascinated, until Mischief tried to flee the constraint. She had just backed off when Mischief tried to shy. She allowed it, so he could see that pulling back would cause discomfort but standing still would relieve it. She had to run forward and push Cole back to keep him from interfering with the object lesson.

"No!" she snapped, forcing herself to ignore the hard muscles flexing beneath her palms. Her proximity didn't seem to affect him in the least. She would die rather than show how hard it was to concentrate on Mischief. "You'll thank me when you need to take care of this horse and he'll stand still for you. You can't coddle two thousand pounds of animal, Cole. You know that! Just give me a chance to do this my way, please. If you want to help, grab a body brush and get to work on your horse as soon as he stands still. He's missed you, so he may be happier if you handle him. But if he shies again just back away and let him learn. Believe me, a few days of this and he'll have learned his lesson."

Cole walked away to pick up a body brush but wheeled, his eyes a mixture of fury, anxiety and pain. "I don't want this!" He closed his eyes, clearly reaching for calm. "Look. I'll deal with him myself from now on. If I have to pay a stable hand to take care of him full-time, I will. You don't know what it's like to be held somewhere against your will. You don't have a clue what it's like when no one understands your pain and your fear. Can you even fathom feeling abandoned by the ones who are supposed to take care of you?"

"Are you talking about Mischief or yourself, big brother?" Hope asked.

Neither of them had heard Hope arrive. They pivoted toward her, and Cole didn't look happy at the intrusion. Or maybe, CJ considered, it was the question that bothered him. For her part, CJ was thrilled. Though she would have been able to handle his anxiety and pain, his fury had ignited her sorry temper. When Cole stared at Hope and didn't deny the truth of her question, CJ's anger faded to nothingness within seconds.

She took a deep breath. *Thank you, Lord, for sending Hope into this situation. Please. Please help me deal with Cole in Your love and Your patience.*

Cole stared at Hope. She had a point. He couldn't say he wasn't overcompensating for Mischief's past or that he hadn't been identifying with the recalcitrant horse. In fact, now that Hope had pointed it out, he had to admit it was a distinct possibility. The truth was, a year ago he'd asked his sister to work with Mischief because he'd known he didn't have the heart to do what was necessary. It wasn't too far a leap from there to his having seen a similarity between his own life and the gelding's. He'd never been mistreated or neglected, of course, but he had been imprisoned and had certainly felt abandoned and misunderstood.

There was another side to the tense scene Hope had interrupted, but CJ seemed oblivious to the problems her nearness caused him. He'd thought he'd swallow his tongue when she slammed her hands into his chest. The feel of those strong, capable hands on him had hit him like the charge from a stun gun. In med school he'd let the teacher zap him to see what an animal would feel and had sworn to never use one. It hadn't felt all that bad this time and that made him uneasy.

Forcing his mind on Mischief, where it belonged, he put away feelings for CJ that only meant trouble. "What's your point?" he asked Hope, trying to still his pounding heart.

"The point, brother mine, is that you don't weigh a tenth what that gelding does. Dad cutting you some slack wouldn't have endangered everyone on the farm, but the slack we've all been giving Mischief could and has. Raymond has a broken arm thanks to us not having had the guts to do the job right."

Cole felt sick. "What happened?"

After Hope explained, Cole looked at CJ, then glanced at the horse, who stood still, though his muscles quivered anxiously beneath his shining hide. Why hadn't she told him? Cole didn't like her methods, but if Mischief had stopped kicking—maybe she knew what she was doing, after all. He'd allow her to move ahead with her program, but he'd watch her work his animal. He'd watch her like a hawk.

The only problem with that was that to watch was to be close. And the closer he was to CJ Larson the closer he wanted to be.

He'd thought to avoid her but he had responsibilities to Mischief, to his family and to Laurel Glen. He couldn't let anything stand in the way of fulfilling the promise he'd made to himself. He would no longer run from the challenge of becoming a part of his own family. He'd no longer run from any challenge.

He glanced at CJ. Except for the one she presented. He'd avoid that one any way left open to him and count himself lucky to escape.

Chapter Six

Cole rode Mischief into the practice ring three weeks after he'd arrived home. He could feel suppressed energy in the gelding's every move. It was clear his boy wanted a good run, and finding himself in the ring was not his idea of an outing. Mischief was in no way a show horse to be satisfied with the precision of riding around a ring. That would require too much discipline.

Though CJ had worked, and was still working, her own particular brand of magic on his rescued horse, Cole didn't kid himself. This animal would always balk at the odd jump just to keep his master on his toes. Mischief had been aptly named.

"He's frisky today," CJ called to him then turned toward the sound of an approaching engine. A shiny, teal pickup pulled up just beyond Stable Four, where the carpenters were working on rebuilding the burned building.

Cole wondered if it was the county building in-
spector, but then a figure right out of the wild West
emerged from the truck. The only thing missing were
the six-guns, chaps and cigarette. Cole rode across
the ring to where CJ had begun to stroll in the
stranger's direction.

An idea—a question—struck with all the devas-
tation of lightning. Had CJ met someone she was
interested in since coming to Laurel Glen?

"Anyone you know?" he asked her, wishing the
answer didn't matter so much. Not even sure why it
did. He'd spent every waking hour of the last three
weeks avoiding as much contact with her as possible.
Why wasn't ignoring her helping curb his attraction?

"No," she replied, looking at him curiously. "I
was about to ask you if he looked familiar to you.
Mind finding out what he wants? Morning has a
loose shoe, and I have a date with Bennet, the new
farrier your dad is trying out."

"Sure thing. I think Mischief here can behave for
a few more minutes."

Cole watched her walk toward the door to Morning's stall that opened into the yard. He couldn't drag
his eyes away for long torturous moments as she
walked across the ring. She had the loose-hipped
walk of a lifelong rider, and it set her long braid
swinging behind her like a shining pendulum.

There was something different about CJ from any
woman he'd ever met. She was strong in a hauntingly
poignant sort of way. Happy and comfortable with
who and what she was and with the body God had

given her, CJ Larson went through each day with enthusiasm and bravery though she had no one in the world.

She also has all the style of the farrier she's gone off to meet, he ruthlessly reminded himself. CJ didn't seem to care what the world thought of her or her lack of femininity. Which, now that he thought about it, really wasn't a lack at all, just a penchant for the most practical clothes known to man. She was a sweet daisy to Elizabeth's exotic orchid, Hope's delicate gardenia, Amelia's elegant rose, and maybe that was CJ's allure. And serenity mixed with a temper so quick you could almost see the sparks when it flared.

She wasn't remotely his type. Of course, Elizabeth—tall, beautiful and stylish—*was* his type, and she didn't move him at all. That was irony at its finest!

Speculation and hypothesis did no good. Neither woman was for him. The woman who could make him take a chance on love didn't exist. His restive mood must have transmitted itself to Mischief, because the horse danced sideways, helping Cole shake off his introspective mood.

He rode across the practice ring and approached the stranger, glad to have something else to think about. "Hi, there. Can I help you?"

The man stared at him then seemed to shake himself from a momentary fog. As if it were habit, he tugged his black Western hat a little lower. "I'm looking for Ross Taggert. Could you point me in his direction?''

The guy reminded Cole of someone, but he couldn't put his finger on who. He was about Cole's age. In fact, come to think of it, they were a near match in every way. Same dark hair. About the same height. Even the same shape of face.

This guy could be family. Maybe that was why he seemed familiar. If he turned out to have blue eyes, he'd look more as if he belonged at Laurel Glen than Cole himself. After all, Cole was the only Taggert ever, as far as he knew, to have brown eyes. It had made him feel more removed from everyone at Laurel Glen after his brown-eyed mother was killed.

"This *is* Laurel Glen, isn't it?" the guy asked.

"That it is," Cole answered, once again shaking himself from introspection. What was wrong with him these days?

After stepping out of the saddle, Cole opened the gate then offered his hand to the stranger. "Welcome to Laurel Glen. I'm Cole Taggert. Is there some way I can help?"

"Name's Jack Alton." He shook Cole's hand, then looked up from their clasped hands.

Cole felt the shock to his toes when their gazes locked. Alton's eyes were a deep sapphire blue. Taggert blue, Aunt Meg called it. Now that they were so close, Cole's brain clicked to the resemblance. Alton looked more like pictures of Cole's grandfather than either he or Ross did. And there was an expectant look in his eye, as if he expected his name to be recognizable.

"What do you want with Ross?" Cole asked.

"Then you don't know who I am? I thought perhaps your father might have mentioned me." The man looked troubled. "We've been talking about the opening you have for a foreman. He was serious—or at least I thought he was. Ross asked me to just drive on in when I got to the area because I wasn't sure how long it would take to drive this far east."

"Well, Dad doesn't tell me a lot about the operation."

"Then I'm not stepping on your toes by applying for the position?"

Cole had to laugh at that. "Me work for my father? No way. We'd kill each other in a week. I'm a vet. I live here and I care for Laurel Glen's animals as part of my practice, but that's as close as I get. It's as close as I want to get. Let me give Dad a yell and see if I can get him down here."

"'ppreciate it," Alton replied with a cowboy kind of nod.

Cole walked away and called Laurel House on his cell phone, then followed the cowboy, who had strolled over to watch Ross's Prize, his father's favorite horse, tear around the southern paddock.

"Dad should be right down. So I guess you're qualified?"

Alton nodded. "I've worked a ranch with my father in Colorado for years, but I needed to get away from the Circle A for a while. Maybe permanently.

Dad and I had differing ideas on the way some things should have been handled.''

Cole could hear strain in Alton's voice and could certainly relate. Every time he had to talk to Ross about anything more important than the weather he felt as if he was negotiating a minefield of dangerous emotion.

Ross approached then, and after briefly introducing the men, Cole stepped back to watch his father and Alton. The resemblance was uncanny. He wanted to say something to warn his father that perhaps there was more to Jack Alton, but Ross didn't seem in the least put off by the man.

Truthfully, if the guy had arrived with a different face, Cole wouldn't have any doubts, either. But there was no getting around the resemblance between this guy and three generations of Taggerts.

It was hard to believe it was coincidence. Alton said he was thirty-one. It was conceivable that Ross could have fathered a child before Cole, but somehow he didn't see his father taking time away from high-school chemistry to sow his wild oats out west. He doubted his grandfather would have extended curfew that far. Cole also couldn't imagine his grandfather fathering a child out of wedlock or not marrying the woman when he was free to do so. Not the tough religious zealot who had banished Aunt Meg from Laurel Glen for the sin of becoming a New York stage actress. It just didn't fit.

Shaking his head, Cole went into the ring and mounted an impatient Mischief. He headed toward

Lavender Hill, his brother-in-law's place, which lay beyond the eastern boundary of Laurel Glen. Maybe Hope knew something about Alton that he didn't.

When Cole returned several hours later with not much more information than he'd left with, the teal pickup was parked next to the small house Harry Donovan had occupied for years. Obviously, Ross had hired the guy.

Cole shrugged. Hope said Alton had responded to Ross's classified ad in *American Horseman* and that his credentials and references had checked out perfectly. She also remembered that Granny Taggert had had a sister who'd married a rancher out west. It was altogether possible that was the connection, but Alton showing up still seemed too coincidental.

Out of the corner of his eye, Cole saw a flash of gold and turned in time to see CJ take Morning over a difficult set of jumps. She and the mare moved with a fluid grace anyone in the equestrian world would envy and applaud, but his heart was pounding with a frightening mix of fear, excitement and pride.

He quickly looked away, toward the foreman's house. He shrugged. *Well, they say everyone has a double. Maybe Grandfather's double or a distant cousin saw the ad for the foreman's position at the right time in his life to make a move.* He sincerely hoped so because he didn't have the energy to worry about why Jack Alton had come to Laurel Glen.

CJ Larson was trouble enough!

Cole jogged down the stairs even though he was purposely late for dinner. There was no use advertising his reluctance to attend one of Amelia's command performances. Her feelings were sort of fragile, which Ross blamed on crazed pregnancy hormones. But whatever the reason, he didn't want to be the one to reduce her to tears.

The reason for his tardiness was the reason for nearly every problem he had right now. CJ was invited to the dinner Amelia had arranged to welcome Jack Alton to Laurel Glen.

With Aunt Meg off on another of her globe-trotting jaunts Cole hadn't had the heart to turn Amelia down. But that didn't mean he was looking forward to the night. He didn't particularly want to spend time with either Alton or CJ. Alton made him uncomfortable, and CJ—well, he refused to put a name to the things CJ made him feel. So he'd delayed coming down until he was sure the meal would be ready to serve and a cell phone call let him know Elizabeth was almost there, which would serve to cut down his exposure to the excruciating before-dinner chat.

He was disappointed when he arrived because neither Alton nor CJ had arrived yet. Amelia smiled at him in a way that let him know she was up to something and that he hadn't kept his disappointment out of his expression.

"Ruth Ann noticed how late you were running so she slowed things down a bit and let everyone know we'd be eating later than usual." She stood and walked to the drink console. "I assume you'd like something to drink while we wait for the others." At the sound of footsteps behind him, Cole tensed and Amelia turned. "Oh, CJ, dear, I was just about to tell Cole that Ruth Ann used the extra time to make a nice frosty pitcher of her strawberry-lemon slushies. It's a favorite of his. Would you like a glass? I know Cole would."

"I'd rather have something stronger," he muttered as he walked across the room, knowing full well his request was a lost cause. The dirty look his father shot him was worth it. Objection to the evening noted, he could grin and bear it. But then he glanced in the mirror and saw CJ in the doorway.

She wore jeans as usual, but these were black, and she wore a simple cream cotton shirt with an embroidered collar. Her hair was pulled back loosely in a long ponytail with some sort of barrette that matched her blouse.

Amelia turned to hand him his drink just as Jack Alton said, "You have a lovely home here, Ross. Your cook, Ruth Ann, sent me on through." He looked around the room, and a frown creased his forehead before he managed to smooth his expression.

Ross stood and made introductions. "That's the family except my sister, Meg, who's traveling. This young lady over here," he continued, motioning to CJ, "is CJ Larson, our trainer. The four of us will meet tomorrow to go over the division of labor."

Cole wondered if anyone else found Jack Alton's appearance a little curious. He glanced at Amelia, who stood staring for a long moment. Her gaze traveled to Ross then to Cole. It was clear the resemblance puzzled her. Shrugging, she turned and gave CJ her slushie. "Can I get you one of Ruth Ann's lemon-strawberry slushies, Mr. Alton?"

"Thank you, ma'am. That'd be fine," he said. Alton wore gray slacks and a black Western-cut shirt with gray piping. He, at least, Cole noted sourly, knew what dress for dinner meant.

Hope motioned Cole away from the drink cabinet and pushed herself to her feet, which was getting to be quite a chore. They met by the front windows. "Glad you could finally join us. And now that I see him, I admit you aren't paranoid. He's a dead ringer for the pictures of Granddad."

Cole nodded. "I tried to tell you."

"Who could he be? More important, why is he here?"

"I don't know, little sis, but you can bet I'm going to find out. Even if I have to call in a marker I swore never to use."

"You're going to ask Jim Lovell to investigate him?"

CJ approached, and Cole signaled Hope that the discussion was over. This was family business, and CJ was *not* family.

"Why do I get the feeling that you don't exactly approve of your father's choice of foreman?" CJ asked quietly.

Cole hated that she could read him so well. "I

never said I don't approve. I don't have to work with the man, nor do I pay his salary."

"He seems like a very nice person. Amelia says he's a committed Christian with excellent personal references."

Cole grimaced. "Oh, that's just peachy."

"You have a bad attitude," she countered.

"I think I'll go chat with my husband and the new man and let you two fight it out," Hope said, not even trying to hide her cheerful grin. "You both do it so well. And for the record, brother dear, you *do* have a bad attitude. Toodles." Hope beat a hasty retreat—at least as fast a one as Hope did anything these days.

"And you're a Pollyanna," Cole said to her retreating back. Then he turned his attention to CJ. "You think going to church is a cure-all for society's problems."

CJ wasn't as reluctant as his sister to pick up the gauntlet. "And you're a cynic," CJ countered, her temper rising. He loved setting it ablaze. Except, of course, that it reminded him of the depth of passion her soul must hold and the fact that he'd like the opportunity to set other portions of her inner being afire, as well.

CJ watched a self-satisfied grin bloom on Cole's handsome face and realized he was baiting her. And she'd almost fallen for it! This couldn't go on. She took a deep breath, said a quick prayer for patience and felt her tension dissolve.

"I know you'd love the opportunity to prove me wrong and debate the merits of a religious life, but there's something I'd like much more," she said quietly. "I'd like to call a truce. I'm here at Laurel Glen to stay, Cole. And I'd like to not have to spar with you at every opportunity. I put in a full day, and having to watch everything I say is extremely tiring. Can't we just put aside our differences and agree to disagree?"

The teasing grin froze on his face, and a look of chagrin settled on his features. "I'm sorry. You're right, of course. I hadn't realized, but I've been doing to you what I do to my dad. You don't deserve it."

CJ longed to point out that Ross didn't deserve it, either, but she held her tongue lest she rock a boat so newly settled in the water. "Thank you. Now that we've settled that, what shall we talk about?"

"Mischief seems safe enough. He's settling down according to Georgie. I'm sorry I haven't had the time to go over his progress with you again, but I've been playing catch-up at the office ever since I got back."

"Checking with me isn't as important as your making the time to spend with him. And you've been doing that—also according to Georgie. And he *is* right. Mischief's doing very well."

"I don't know how to thank you. Amelia said you went to bat for him when Dad was all set to make me find somewhere else to board him."

"I just had to set Ross straight when he misunderstood the accident Ray and Mischief had."

"Yeah, right. If it had been any other animal on the placc, he'd have listened before assuming. He never wanted Mischief here, but he sure took Demon from Jeff and Hope quickly enough."

When Cole glanced at Ross, who stood chatting with Amelia and Jack across the room, CJ saw the hurt in his eyes. She was nearly positive the hurt explained his anger. She put her hand on Cole's forearm.

"If Mischief had been anyone else's horse, he'd have been out of here months ago. Your father was living in fear of having to tell you it was time to give up on Mischief. You weren't there to see his relief when I fully explained that Ray's broken arm was an accident. As for Demon, look at your sister. Do you want her saddle breaking a high-spirited animal like Demon right now?"

She didn't have to wait for his answer. It was in his expression and his stance. "Remember your reaction to seeing Demon? Your father went six shades of pale when we backed him out of the trailer. Jeff said he'd never seen the horse that killed your mother but that he knew this one looked like him the second he saw Ross's reaction. By then it was too late. If we'd loaded Demon back up, Hope would have insisted he go to Lavender Hill."

Cole glanced at Ross again. "He *was* worried about the black and he *did* want my opinion. It's just that…"

"It's habit for you to second-guess his motives, isn't it?"

"I guess it is," he admitted with a self-conscious shrug. "But you don't understand."

"Oh, you are so right on that score. I don't understand a father and son who can't discuss the weather half the time without questioning each other's motives. You really have to learn to talk to each other."

"Like I said. You don't understand. He questions everything I do or say. He always assumes the worst."

She was a boat rocker after all. "And you don't?" she countered. "Have you ever seen hamsters running around on those little wheels? That's what you remind me of. Both of you. Chasing after something you'll never reach because you can't step far enough away to see how futile an exercise you're trapped in. You two are so afraid to widen the rift with one honest conversation that you're both willing to let your relationship drift further apart."

Cole's jaw tensed. "I came home willing to talk, and he started sniping at me within days."

"And you didn't snipe right back?"

That question didn't need an answer, either. It, too, was in his eyes. "I can't undo the past, and that's what he wants," he defended. "I admit I did some pretty stupid things, but I was a kid."

"I'd heard rumors to that effect," she put in with a smile and a chuckle. She could see him now. A young, dark James Dean.

"You can laugh. You don't have someone mentioning your mistakes constantly as if they happened yesterday. You were probably a model child.''

"Not so. Remember I told you my parents were killed in a plane crash while I was a senior in high school? Well, I wasn't with my parents on that trip because I'd played hooky to ride into the woods to a destination where I was forbidden to go.''

"You didn't do the kind of things I did.''

"That's not my point. When they told me I had to stay home with Grandpa as punishment, I said some childish, stupid things. I thank God every day that He gave me the grace to chase them to the car that morning to apologize for the things I said. I still wasn't allowed to go along, but at least we didn't part in anger. Had we, it would have been forever.''

"I know I was wrong, and I've said so. You'd think he'd be happy just to see me come as far as I have. But no. He wants the impossible. He wants me to somehow undo it all.''

"And you don't want that? What is it you want of him? Don't you want him to undo past mistakes just as badly? Talk to him, Cole. Find a way to put peace between you. You never know how much time you have. I speak from a lot of experience.''

"And speaking of a lot of experience,'' Hope said under her breath as she returned to her brother's side. "Elizabeth just arrived. I wasn't aware Amelia had invited her.''

"Your claws are showing, princess.'' From his gritted teeth and biting tone it was clear that *princess* was not a term of endearment. "Sheath them,'' Cole ordered after a tense pause, then he stalked toward his lovely guest.

"She's very nice. Why don't you like her?" CJ asked, curious.

Hope sighed, and her shoulders sagged. "Because I'm a terrible person. She used to date Jeff, and I'm fat and dumpy."

"Untrue," Jeff Carrington said as he sauntered up and kissed Hope on the cheek. "We were only friends. And you are all that is beautiful and lovely to me, and I love you."

Seconds later, Cole, his arm around Elizabeth, led her over. "CJ, you've met Elizabeth."

"It's good to see you again," CJ told Elizabeth.

The blond beauty's answering smile was just as genuine now as the day they'd met. CJ couldn't help liking her even if Cole smiled easily in her presence when all CJ could do was make him mad.

"I'm so glad you survived Ross's trial period," Elizabeth said. "I was afraid you wouldn't get a chance to even unhitch your trailer."

"I almost didn't. Cole convinced Mr. Taggert to give me a chance."

"From what I can see of Mischief and his better behavior, I'd say that was a wise move."

"Just stay away from mud puddles around him," Hope advised. "CJ hasn't had a chance to work on his mischievous streak."

Elizabeth laughed. "Women pay hundreds for mud baths. I got one for free." She patted Cole's hand where it rested on her shoulder. "I told Cole at the time it was no problem, but he didn't believe me.''

''A mud puddle on May first is hardly a luxury. You were chilled to the bone by the time Aunt Meg got you changed.''

''Yes, but my skin was so much softer,'' she teased, making them all laugh. It was easy to see why Cole cared for her. She was very sweet, for all her sophistication. She was, in fact, all the things CJ wasn't. And had never wanted to be.

Chapter Seven

CJ found herself thinking about her conversation with Cole on and off the next day. Mostly, though, she thought about Cole. About his tall good looks. About the charm he showed nearly everyone but her. About the storm clouds that had gathered in his beautiful dark eyes during dinner when Ross made a disparaging remark about Mischief to Jack Alton.

Luckily, before dinner had a chance to deteriorate into a shouting match between father and son, an emergency call came in and Cole had to rush off to care for a sick cow. CJ didn't know why two such wonderful men couldn't stop sparring long enough to see how much they loved each other. Hope, it was clear, had come to the end of her rope with them, and Amelia wasn't far behind. It was no wonder Meg Taggert spent most of her time jetting all over the world. Living in that house must be like living in a war zone.

CJ wished she could help. She'd thought she'd gotten through to Cole before Elizabeth arrived, but when talk turned to business at dinner and Ross brought up Mischief as a problem to be watched, Cole's hackles had risen. Of course, Ross should have been aware of what his son's reaction would be to criticism of the animal. He should have waited to explain the problems with Mischief and how Ray had been injured. He certainly could have mentioned Demon's need of familiar faces before discussing the slight ongoing problems with Cole's baby.

It looked as if the only way to get them really talking might be to lock them in a room together with a referee. Who would be insane enough to volunteer for such hazardous duty was a mystery, though. One thing was certain—it wouldn't be her!

CJ checked her watch and frowned. Where had the day gone? Shaking her head, she got to her feet, picked up her helmet and went to saddle Morning. A good run was what she needed to clear her head of thoughts of sparkling onyx eyes, a lady-killer grin and muscular arms she wished had guided her across the room last night instead of Elizabeth Boyer.

Cole closed the file and tossed it into his out bin. He looked at the clock and winced. He had no more calls to make, no more patients to see. Not much filing needed to be done, and that wasn't his job. He couldn't stall any longer. It was time to go home. And that meant the possibility of seeing CJ.

He had managed to avoid her, for the most part,

during the last couple of weeks, at least until last night's dinner. It hadn't been an easy task. She seemed to be everywhere. He rode at dawn when he knew she was briefing the men. He came in and rubbed Mischief down when he knew she'd gone to her little cabin to eat breakfast. He made sure he was gone from the stables by the time she returned. The only reason he was so on edge about her tonight was that he'd been forced to spend all that time with her last evening.

She was so compelling and earnest. He'd spent the entire night distracted by her presence even with Elizabeth next to him. He'd been on edge, so when his father started explaining Mischief's problems, Cole's reaction had been out of proportion. Then the phone had rung and saved him from sitting across from CJ and making an idiot of himself because of it. He'd never before been so happy to have a sick cow interrupt his dinner.

Cole stood and pulled his keys out of his pocket to lock up. As he closed the door behind him, the phone rang. At nearly six o'clock it probably meant an emergency—a reprieve. He didn't know whether to be relieved or ashamed for being glad someone had a problem with one of their animals.

"Chester County Animal Clinic. Taggert speaking."

"Cole, it's Hope. Are you going to be here soon?"

"Where here? Laurel House or Lavender Hill? Did I forget a dinner invitation?"

"No. I'm at Laurel Glen. We've got a problem."

Cole frowned. Hope sounded upset. "I was just leaving. What's up?"

"It's CJ's mare. She doesn't look good. CJ's putting her in her stall now. Would you stop on your way in and take a look at her?" Hope let out a little gasp. "Morning just stumbled. I don't like these symptoms."

"Talk to me. What symptoms?" he asked as he started throwing gear into a leather bag.

"She's listless, stumbling, and her hind limbs seem weak."

"I'm on my way." He didn't like that combo, either.

Nearly two hours later Cole backed out of Morning's stall and slid the bolt home. He turned to face CJ, who stood next to Hope, apprehension written in her stance and expression. He wished he had better news. He wished he didn't think what he thought.

If there was one thing Laurel Glen didn't need, it was negative publicity, and if Morning had contracted what he thought, there wouldn't be any avoiding it. Laurel Glen would once again be on the evening news, because West Nile Virus was big news. Because the media loved playing up the danger it posed to humans, Laurel Glen would be at the forefront of a county-wide panic. It had happened in Jersey just last year.

But it was CJ who stood to lose the most. The mare was the only remaining tie to her past and her family other than the bunch of junk he'd helped her move into the cabin. He could put off telling everyone what he suspected until he got off the phone with the National Veterinary Services Laboratories, but once he alerted the NVSL and shipped the samples to Ames, Iowa, he'd have no choice but to tell CJ and his father what he suspected.

"It looks like a viral infection," he told her. Time enough to break her heart later. "I want to move Morning to the clinic in the barn. She'll do better in a lower stress environment. Hope, why don't you take CJ over and show her where I'll treat her mare. I'll have Georgie and Jack bring Morning over."

"But—" CJ started to protest.

"Let's just take this one step at a time. Okay?" he suggested gently.

"Okay," CJ agreed, sounding lost and terribly worried. Cole's heart ached for her as he watched her leave after a last anxious glance at Morning.

"So what's this virus?" Jack Alton asked. "It looks like some form of encephalitis, EEE or WEE."

Cole shook his head. "Morning was vaccinated against those. You're the foreman, so I hate to order you around, but there are some things I need done. I want everyone here wearing insect repellant. Make sure it has deet in it. And they need to spray their clothes as well as any exposed skin. In the morning, you need to have every available worker looking for any standing water on the place and eliminating it. Have them take a sample of the water first and label it. Let me know where it came from. Use the grid map of the farm on the wall in Dad's office to mark locations and correlate samples. The more of this we do on our own the less the FDA will need to be tromping all over the place. If you can't eliminate a body of standing water, take the sample and we'll use spray on it. Jersey had good results with that last summer. Oh, and if you find a dead bird, bag it and bring it in.''

Alton stared at him. "Mind sharing what you suspect? I'd like to know what I'm dealing with. From that last request, I'd say it isn't anything pretty.''

"I'm afraid it's West Nile Virus.''

Alton winced. "I've heard of it, but I don't know much about it. Except for how fatal it is. That much I got from the national news.''

"We still don't know all that much about it, but it isn't necessarily fatal. It's a new disease that's spread by infected mosquitoes, and people are easily panicked. The virus multiplies in the horse's blood system, crosses the blood-brain barrier and infects the brain,'' Cole explained. "It interferes with normal central nervous system function and causes inflammation of the brain itself. Luckily, it isn't communicable except through mosquito bites.''

They both looked around. "Maybe I should see what I can do about mosquito-proofing the buildings, too,'' Alton suggested.

"It's never gotten this close so it never mattered. I could be wrong. I hope I am, but I think it's worth the precautions.''

Alton's mood was as grave as his. "But you don't think you're wrong, do you?''

Cole shook his head.

"It's a real shame. That's one fine-looking mare."

Cole offered no comment. He was on his way to the barn when he saw Ross heading his way. It looked as if he already knew there was a problem.

"I just saw Hope take CJ into the clinic. They both looked upset. What's up?"

"Morning's picked up something. Alton and Georgie are moving her now. It isn't anything simple. I have to call FedEx to get some samples to the lab then I'll know for sure."

"What lab?" Ross asked.

Cole took a deep breath. "The NVSL in Ames, Iowa. Dad, I think it's West Nile."

Ross blinked in surprise. "Don't you think that's an overreaction? There hasn't been a case anywhere in the area. Wayne's as close as it's gotten. Do you have any idea of the panic this could cause if it gets out? Are you trying to finish what Donovan started?"

Cole felt his stomach knot. "It wouldn't occur to you that I might know what I'm talking about, would it? Causing a panic is the last thing I want. Look, Dad, I have an obligation to public safety that supercedes my loyalty to Laurel Glen's business. And look at it this way. Maybe the measures I've just outlined with Alton will minimize the risk to the animals and the people living here. Now if you'll excuse me, I have to get a DMSL IV running into that mare to minimize the swelling in her brain."

CJ and Hope helped settle Morning in the clinic stall. It had interlocking rubber mats for bedding and on the half walls of the stall. The other walls were bright white and appointed with stainless steel cabinets. It looked like a small animal hospital. It should have made her feel better because it meant Morning would get the best of care, but the high-tech look left her nervous. Her precious mare was so sick she needed all this special care!

Cole rushed in and went to a cabinet. He took out an IV bag and yards of tubing coiled like telephone cord. After setting them on a steel tray on wheels he moved to a sink and scrubbed his hands. The set of his jaw said he was furious.

"What's wrong with Morning, Cole?" she asked.

"I'm not sure. I'm going to take some samples and send them to a lab. There's no use speculating till I get the results."

"I have to know what you're treating her for. Please. I need to know."

"Look, I promise you I'll do everything I can."

His clear reluctance told CJ Morning's condition was as serious as she'd feared. But was it hopeless?

"I can tell it has you angry. What is it?"

"I'm furious with my father, not at what's wrong with the mare. It looks to me like some form of virus. The trouble is it's already gotten past the blood-brain barrier. I'm putting her on an IV drip, which should help."

CJ wanted to scream at him to tell her the truth. "Name it!" she ordered. "Just give it a name. What is your best guess? What kind of virus?"

"I'm about ninety-nine percent sure it's encephalitis in some form. What kind will be up to the tests to determine.''

"Cole, are the other horses in danger from Morning?" Hope asked.

"No. I wanted her here for her sake. This isn't a quarantine situation. I'll call Jeff later, though, about some precautions you should all take. The most important will be to eliminate any standing water that could breed mosquitoes and for everyone to use a repellant like this one with thirty-five percent deet.''

Hope took the can Cole held out to her and frowned. ''Insect spray? I'm not sure this is good for the baby.''

Cole frowned. "I'll have someone bring your car down. I'm not sure either you or Amelia should use it. Stay indoors at dawn and dusk till we're sure what this is. Give Amelia a call and warn her. It might not be any more dangerous than any other strain of encephalitis to you two or the babies, but there's a risk even with that.''

"It's West Nile, isn't it?" CJ asked, suddenly sure. Morning had several of the symptoms she'd seen last summer on a Web site about the disease. Cole was trying to protect her.

"I'm not sure," he answered on a deep sigh. "Please don't panic. Just let me start her IV and get the samples sent. I promise I'll do all I can for her. It isn't necessarily fatal even if it is West Nile, and you can bet I won't destroy her unless there's no hope.''

CJ closed her eyes and said a quick prayer asking

God to guide Cole and strengthen Morning. Then she slid to the floor in the corner and watched Cole as he worked. His movements were competent and assured as he started two IV lines, then packed up the samples he'd mentioned.

Hope called an overnight delivery company to pick them up, then she left. Cole asked CJ all sorts of questions about Morning's last several days. He checked and rechecked the mare's breathing and reflexes. Then she heard him on the phone with a doctor at the Iowa lab. He rattled off airway bill numbers, the number of samples and a bunch of medical terms she was sure were Morning's symptoms but in words she didn't understand. He'd no sooner gotten off the phone than the overnight shipping company came to get the samples.

As the courier left Ross arrived. "Are you sure there isn't another way?" Ross asked without preamble.

"I told you, Dad, I'm handling this by the book. I don't have a choice and, if I did, I'd still do it this way. I'm sorry if this hurts business. There's no reason it should, other than ignorance of the dangers. I worry more about how this animal got infected. There are people involved here. One of us could be down with this and not Morning."

"I'm, ah, I'm sorry if I seemed to doubt you out there. I just can't believe something else is conspiring to destroy this place."

Cole leaned against a counter. He looked tired. "I can't, either." He scrubbed his hand across his face, and his five o'clock shadow whispered against his palm. "If I get a few minutes, I'll talk to everyone and coach them on how to handle any media questions. Maybe we can minimize the damage by educating the public with our answers."

"Good idea. Well, I'll leave you to it. CJ, I hope everything turns out okay. Don't worry about anything else right now. We'll all pick up the slack for you."

CJ nodded and rested her head against the wall. She closed her eyes and fought the tears that wanted so desperately to flow.

Oh, please don't let her die.

Cole came over and sank to the floor next to her. Morning had long since done the same in the stall. "You told Hope she was a gift from your parents. What was the occasion?"

CJ felt her lips tip into a slight smile. She kept her eyes closed, trying to remember every aspect of that day. It had been a sunny spring day. The kind with summer on the breeze and the sun playing peekaboo with the high, fluffy clouds.

"It was for high school graduation. I got her early because Daddy couldn't wait. I was always thankful for that or they'd have been gone before I got her. Daddy had seen her at an auction, and Mom said all he could talk about was how she matched my hair. He bought her black tack to match my black velvet riding outfit."

"I'm glad your gift of a horse turned out better than mine." Cole's voice was every bit as hushed as hers had been, but his pain was a tangible thing that hung in the air. "The black Dad bought me was beautiful, too, but Dynamite got twisted somewhere along the line, or he was just born warped. I haven't celebrated a birthday since. He threw me and stood over me pawing the ground as if to say, 'I could grind you to dust.' It was in his eyes. I can't explain how I knew, but it didn't matter. No one would listen when I tried to tell them."

CJ opened her eyes and looked at him. She didn't know why he'd decided to talk to her. Was this his version of bedside manner or could he not help himself because yet another run-in with his father had opened up the floodgates of Cole's pain? Whatever the reason, CJ wasn't going to let the opportunity pass her by.

"How old were you?" she asked, longing to keep him talking.

"Fifteen." He said it like a sigh on the wind—so much anguish wrapped up in that single word.

She'd known the answer but she wanted to encourage him to keep talking. If she thought about the scars of his past, she didn't have to ponder hers. "I guess it might have been hard for your father to admit you knew more about a horse than he did," she said, hoping to draw him out.

"For a long time I thought that was a factor. But I also thought something a lot worse, with Donovan's warped help. He had me thinking Dad had let Dynamite kill Mom so he'd get all her parents' money."

"Having gotten to know Ross even a little, that doesn't sound possible."

"It's not. He wouldn't harm a fly. With all the stunts I pulled, in fact, not once in my life did he raise a hand to either Hope or me. And he'd always been open to my ideas and feelings."

"Do you know what made that day so different?"

Cole nodded, his lips pursed slightly. He shifted and dropped his arm on his upraised knee before explaining. "I'd overheard an argument between my parents the night before Mom was killed. I could only hear snatches of what they were saying, but divorce and an affair were part of what I did hear. She was so wonderful that I assumed it was Dad making demands and confessions."

"And then she was killed and you started getting in trouble. Was it to spite your father? Or was it self-destructive?" she asked, remembering what Hope had said the day CJ arrived.

"Both. I blamed him. I blamed me."

"You blame God, still."

He raised an eyebrow as if to say she wasn't getting a rise out of him that night. "Turns out God was the only one who had control over what happened that day. It took a year for me to start doubting that Dad had either deliberately caused her death or at least let her die. I had myself convinced Dad took his own sweet time getting a rifle to kill Dynamite and save Mom. But no new woman showed up in our lives so I tested the theory."

There was a faraway look in his eyes that was

steeped in the pain of past events. Events he'd been too young to fully understand. "I was so wrong. Of course, I've since learned that I didn't arrive at my false conclusion alone. I was so stupid! I still don't know how Dad got back with that rifle as fast as he did, but I finally know why I thought he was slow. Donovan manipulated me while pretending not to believe the conclusion he led me to.

"In discounting that theory, I tossed out what I'd heard about a third party being involved in the trouble between them, thinking that if it wasn't Dad, I'd heard wrong and it had just been a divorce they'd been arguing about."

"What happened next?"

"I went a little crazy, I guess. That's the night I pulled my last big stunt. I stole a police cruiser and went flying up and down the roads, sirens blaring. I wanted the whole county to know Dad couldn't control me."

"I don't understand. I'd have thought knowing your father wasn't a murderer would have been a relief."

"Except that if Dad didn't delay saving her, then she might have ridden the black hoping to be killed. I assumed she loved Dad too much to go on without him. That was wrong, too, as it turns out. I only learned recently that it was Mom asking for a divorce. She confessed to having an affair, but Dad didn't tell anyone. And no one knew it was Donovan, our foreman, she was carrying on with. She was going to leave us behind and go off with him."

"And Donovan turned out to be the one responsible for the sabotage around here last summer."

Cole nodded. "He's in prison now. We caught him after he monkeyed with Amelia's car, and he told Dad that Mom rode Dynamite to try make up for what she'd done. She thought if she could patch up the argument between us, he'd forgive her."

"If you know all this, why are the two of you still at odds?"

Cole tilted his head to the side and gazed at her, his eyes narrowed in thought. He had such beautiful eyes. "I don't know," he said with a shake of his head. "All I wanted when I came home was to try to figure out how to get back the relationship we once had, but it isn't happening. I think he's sorry he's my father. I was a terrible embarrassment to him. That wild ride did the trick on that score. He said it often enough when I first got home. I got the message loud and clear."

"Has he said it lately?"

Once again, Cole frowned. She was relieved to see that he was truly bothered by his poor relationship with Ross.

"Not since Donovan tried to pin the blame on me," he continued. "Dad thought it was me, in the beginning, before he started defending me. The night the stable burned, he went ballistic and more or less decked a state cop who tried to stop Dad from talking to me."

"That sounds pretty fatherly to me. And I heard him apologize to you earlier. It sounds like all this arguing is nothing more than a bad habit between you and your father. Maybe you two should be locked in a room till you come out with some sort of understanding.''

Cole shot her a crooked grin and chuckled. ''I hadn't realized that approach was on the table.''

CJ tried to smile, but with Morning shifting restlessly nearby she knew she didn't pull it off too convincingly. ''Call it a hunch, but I think I could convince your sister and aunt of its merits real easily.''

He smirked and stood. ''I'd imagine you could. Very easily.''

She watched him check Morning, change IV bags and change the frequency of the drip. She'd figured him out. He'd been willing to expose his pain to take her mind off her own. It had worked—for a little while, anyway.

''Is Morning going to make it?'' She couldn't help asking.

He regarded her steadily, his dark eyes solemn. There was no bantering or obfuscation now. ''If I have anything to say about it, she will.''

Chapter Eight

Cole wished he could give CJ more of a promise than that he'd give saving the mare his best effort, but he knew she'd see through the lie. And to promise more would have been just that. He couldn't even say the odds were in Morning's favor since statistics were so sporadic and inconclusive. And it was clear from her bleak expression CJ knew the truth. All of it. He didn't know when he'd been more frustrated.

Compelled to at least offer comfort, Cole finished adjusting the drip on Morning's IV and went to CJ's side. He'd done all he could do for the mare, and her owner seemed to need him more right then. His heart ached as he watched her hug her legs and rest her cheek on her knees, her gaze fixed on the mare in the clinic's stall.

"I'm sorry I can't promise she'll survive. But she's young, and she's strong," he said as he squatted next to CJ.

CJ nodded, but her lower lip quivered and her eyes filled with tears. "She's all I have left in the world. Oh, please, dear Lord, don't let me lose her, too."

For once, he wasn't going to ridicule or belittle her childlike faith. He sincerely wished God would answer her prayer, though Cole had little hope that He would even notice the little drama being played out in a barn in Pennsylvania.

What he wanted to do instead was take her in his arms and comfort her, but he didn't dare. He'd gone to a lot of effort to avoid this woman. It hadn't really worked. She drew him like a fly to honey—a moth to flame. She looked at him, her golden-brown eyes anguished, and Cole was lost. He sank to the floor next to her and wrapped her in his arms. She leaned into him and went boneless as if the effort to sit was beyond her.

Feeling utterly selfish because nothing had ever felt so right, Cole tucked her head beneath his chin and inhaled the fresh spring scent of her hair. "So your parents died right after giving you Morning. You were what? Seventeen? Eighteen?"

"Seventeen. My grandfather helped me keep the farm going for five years but then he took sick. By the time he died two years later, I had to declare bankruptcy. The good-old-boy network didn't give me much choice."

"What exactly went wrong? You seem so competent. Was it the business side of the farm you couldn't handle?"

She shook her head a little, as if a vehement protest was beyond her. "I'd had a hard time keeping us up and running at full speed while I took care of Grandpa that last two years. Then he died, and even though I'd been the only Larson anyone saw around the operation for years, I was suddenly too young to handle the responsibility of my animals, other peoples' animals and rider safety. Business dropped off, and I got a few payments behind on the mortgage. With Grandpa gone, within months I had inheritance taxes to pay."

"Dad had that same problem when I was a kid," Cole told her. "He had to take out a mortgage to pay them, from what I hear. I know he was always working when we were young. So things were getting tight?"

"Tight," she said with just a little disgust in her voice. "I already had a mortgage my dad had taken out for a couple of new stable buildings. Then the government started breathing down my neck for the taxes. I paid them, but couldn't pay the mortgage, too. The president of the bank had gone to school with my father, and he was as sorry as he could be, but he had to foreclose. It was for my own good, anyway, don't you know? Nearly everyone in town thought I was wasting my life. Poor Charlie Larson. No life or prospects with that millstone called Morning Star Farms around her neck. My grandfather's lawyer said my only option after the bank foreclosed was to file for bankruptcy. I suppose it *was* my only option by then."

"If your parents and grandparents had a lawyer,

why didn't he do something to protect you from some of the taxes? He could have done so much.''

''Ah. Yes. Mr. Country Lawyer. Unfortunately, he was either an idiot or working with the guy who bought the place at auction. I've always voted a tie on that one. I could never decide if he'd been smart enough to be able to look incompetent or if he was just that bad a lawyer. I only managed to keep Morning because a neighbor bought her at the auction then came to me and told me I could buy her back any time I had the money.''

''You couldn't have lost more if you'd just walked away. As I said, my dad faced pretty much the same problems when his father died just before I was born. Dad was only nineteen, but at least he didn't have the mortgage problems already. Even though the inheritance taxes on this place were enormous, he was able to get a loan.''

''He seems like a good man, your father.'' She looked up, her face within inches of his, her brown eyes all luminous behind the tears that filled them. ''His son's a good man, too.''

Cole wanted to run. Wanted to hold her close all night. Wanted too much, including to kiss her. Instead, coward that he was, he elected to hide behind a poor, sick mare who needed her rest. He patted CJ's shoulder and eased her out of his arms. ''I need to check Morning's vitals,'' he said and climbed to his feet. But he could only fuss over the mare for so long.

This time, when he sat down, Cole kept a good

three or four feet between them. "Try to sleep," he advised. "It's going to be a long night." He put his head back and closed his eyes.

Just past four in the morning Cole heard Morning grow anxious. Within minutes the seizures started. He was ready to add phenobarbital and corticosteroids to her treatment when CJ scrambled to her feet and rushed into the stall.

"She was resting so comfortably. What happened?" she insisted on knowing.

How to tell her this was almost inevitable? Cole wondered as he measured out the appropriate doses of each drug. "It's the effect of the brain swelling," he explained, trying to sound matter of fact. "I'd hoped this wouldn't happen, but it isn't unusual."

Morning's one leg flailed out and smashed into the stall wall, her body quaking and thrashing. CJ let out a cry of distress. "Don't do any more, Cole," she said, sniffling and fighting tears. "She's suffering too much. I'm being selfish. You have to put her down."

He took CJ by her shoulders. "Look at me," he ordered, and braced himself for the impact of her golden, tear-filled eyes. The bracing didn't work, but he studiously ignored his heart's reaction. "You asked me to trust you to take care of Mischief. You promised you wouldn't be cruel, and I doubted you at first. But I'm glad I listened. Now I'm asking for the same amount of trust from you about your animal."

His resolve began to slip. He wanted nothing more

than to wrap her in his arms and take away her pain and fear. But he couldn't. Not and survive whole. He knew that much about himself. Instead of traveling further into dangerous territory, he tried to lighten the atmosphere with a cocky grin. Maybe if he didn't seem concerned, she wouldn't be.

"Well," he said, continuing his plea for trust, "it wouldn't hurt if you'd take a little less time to come around than I did. And maybe you could be less of an idiot about it in the meantime, too."

She didn't even crack a smile. Just stared at him, melting his heart with those big, luminous, twenty-two-karat eyes of hers. "Listen to me, sweetheart. I wouldn't put her through this if I didn't think it would be worth it in the end. Morning wouldn't want you to give up on her. Now tell me to get to work."

CJ sniffled and blinked. "Okay. Go. Get to work," she said, her voice all but a sob.

Morning stabilized around eight. He'd slept maybe two hours on and off all night, and Cole doubted CJ got even that much rest.

By ten the investigators had arrived. By noon Morning's illness hit the television news. He'd coached the handlers and other farm workers, and Ross stopped by to say that several of their calm, deliberate comments on the lack of communicability of the disease had made it into the TV and newspaper reports. Unfortunately, there were also reporter comments on old news. The fire. The arrest of Donovan for murder and attempted murder. His recent conviction.

CJ left for a while to make sure none of the other animals were down. Cole took advantage of her absence by giving the mare another dose of the steroids that reduced brain swelling. They were extremely dangerous medications, and everyone who worked around horses knew it. At that point, though, they were a course of treatment he deemed necessary. He just had to be mindful that if he used them too long— and that time frame was different in every animal— he could cause a painfully devastating condition commonly referred to as founder.

He also talked to several experts, vets from New Jersey and New York who had pulled horses through West Nile. They all agreed that the mare had a better than average chance of survival with the supportive course of treatment Cole had chosen no matter how severe her symptomatology. Apparently, the severity of the symptoms had little to do with the ultimate outcome. Some animals showing no outward signs had suddenly dropped dead, and others appearing sick recovered. That was the good news. The bad news was that from what he'd read on the Internet and learned by calling the University of Pennsylvania's School of Veterinary Medicine, if the mare survived, she might never be the same. Which was the reason for the euthanasia advice that was suddenly flowing in from all quarters.

With all the talk of putting her down, he didn't feel comfortable leaving Morning to anyone else's care. He had his receptionist reschedule regular appointments and hand off any emergencies to the same large practice he'd called on when he'd gone to California to settle his affairs. For some reason they felt entitled to call and hand out free advice, just like everyone else. When the fourth member of the practice called, Cole refused to go to the phone.

So E. Jonathan Darnelle, DVM, showed up at Laurel Glen's clinic to spout his opinion.

Cole looked up from checking the IV drip to find him standing a few feet inside the clinic. Unfortunately, Morning chose that moment to have another seizure. As Cole rushed to get another dose of phenobarbital and steroids to add to the regular drip he'd been using to keep the mare hydrated, Darnelle stepped in his way to stop him from getting to the drug cabinet.

"This is an abomination. How can you put that poor animal through this?"

Teeth gritted, Cole said, "Get out of my way. And out of my clinic while you're on the move."

Darnelle moved, but didn't stop talking. Nor did he leave. "How can you do this to a poor, dumb creature?"

Cole opened the drug cabinet and stopped to glare at the society boy he'd had so many run-ins with in high school. He saw very little difference between the obnoxious boy he'd known in high school and the man before him—other than more height and less hair. "That mare probably has more intelligence in her left ear than you do," Cole told him.

"You have the same smart mouth you had as a kid. I should have known you hadn't changed."

Cole continued to look at the other vet. "Nope," he quipped. "Haven't changed a bit. But neither have you. You're still the same officious know-it-all you were back in school."

Then he dismissed Darnelle from his thoughts and turned his attention to the thrashing mare. Cole grabbed the medication he needed and went to work.

Darnelle ignored Cole's comment. "Does the owner know there's every possibility that brain damage is being done each time that horse seizes? Or how dangerous those steroids are? Look at the lines on this mare. She's championship quality. What possible good will that animal be to the owner after this?"

Cole turned. "What good?"

"That mare will be nothing but a burden and miserable if she can't compete! Look at her. She was bred for competition."

"No, she wasn't. She doesn't compete now. Never has. And as for being a burden, there will always be a pasture and a stall for her here at Laurel Glen, free of charge. A horse doesn't need to have a higher purpose to be happy. She isn't a person. If she never does more than chomp grass and love her owner, she's fulfilled her *purpose*."

Cole was confident he'd spoken not only for Laurel Glen's offer for the mare's future upkeep but also for CJ, Morning and their relationship. The mare was clearly willing to fight this thing for CJ. He could see the will to live in the palomino's eyes.

"Are you an expert?" CJ demanded as she

stormed in, having heard his confrontation with the other vet.

About an hour earlier she'd gone down the hall to her office to lie down on the sofa for a few minutes. When Morning started to seize again in the middle of Cole's confrontation with Darnelle, Cole had forgotten she was in the building. He braced himself, ready for her to withdraw her trust.

"I—I graduated fiftieth in my class from the University of Pennsylvania," Darnelle answered.

CJ smiled, and Cole's heart fell. She was going to listen to Darnelle.

"That's very impressive," she said, but he noticed her voice had a mocking lilt. "Credentials don't mean you know what's best in this case. How many cases of West Nile Virus or even encephalitis have you treated?"

Darnelle hesitated. "Well, none to speak of, but I studied up on it when it showed up in the tristate area."

"And you think Cole hasn't? You have some nerve coming here, to his family's private clinic, pretending to know what you're talking about when you clearly don't have a clue! And for the record, he's right! If Morning never does more than eat grass, at least she's alive and enjoying herself."

With Darnelle beating a hasty retreat, Cole found himself smiling for the first time in hours. Before he could get too comfortable or even thank CJ for her support and trust, Morning tried to stand, and pulled out her IV when she couldn't. She gave him a good

kick in the shoulder when he got close to check if
she'd hurt herself. As he knelt next to the mare, grit-
ting his teeth in pain, Cole was cheered. That good
solid kick came from the limb most affected. He
found himself foolishly hoping the little darling had
used enough power to break his shoulder!

Before the mare could do any more damage in her
quest to stand, Cole had CJ call Georgie, and they
got the mare in a sling to help her stand. He'd
planned to get Morning on her feet soon anyway. He
worried that she might develop colic because she
wasn't eating. After he had her on her feet he inserted
a nasal gastric tube so he could introduce a slurry of
food into her stomach to keep her digestive system
moving.

Word came just about twenty-four hours later that
preliminary findings at the lab in Ames, Iowa, con-
firmed that Morning had contracted West Nile Virus.
With the confirmation came yet another storm of
controversy over Cole's efforts to save the mare.

There were also the investigative team's findings
that there was no contamination in any standing water on either Taggert or Carrington land. The culprit
was the pool on the estate owned by Elizabeth
Boyer's father. The pool had not been opened this
year and had provided a breeding ground for the
deadly mosquitoes. Reginald Boyer offered no explanation for the poor maintenance. Cole knew from
a few things Elizabeth said that the man had fallen
on financial hard times, though he refused help and

wouldn't allow his daughter to use her degree for more than volunteer work.

To add insult to injury, when interviewed, Boyer tried to shift the focus off himself and onto Cole and his "ridiculous waste of resources on an animal that should be put down." Cole had already accepted Elizabeth's unnecessary apology, knowing he'd never get one from her father.

For the next three days, nursing a separated shoulder and wearing a splint that got in the way constantly, Cole took turns with CJ keeping watch over Morning. Just past dawn the fourth day, Cole heard a muffled sound coming from the down the hall. Instantly awake, he staggered out of CJ's office, where he'd been sleeping on the old sofa. In the clinic, he found Morning trying out the strength in her left hindquarter, the one most affected by the virus.

CJ was sound asleep, not alerted by the hushed sound, so he let her sleep. After giving the mare a thorough going-over, however, Cole decided his was news worth waking her for. Morning still couldn't stand without the aid of the sling, but she'd clearly passed the crisis. He hunkered down next to CJ and whispered her name.

Her lashes fluttered open, revealing her golden eyes, hazy with exhaustion. Worry banished the soft, unfocused look in seconds. "What's wrong? Is she worse again? Oh, I'm so sorry I fell asleep!"

"Relax. Nothing's wrong. In fact, something's right. That mare of yours is one tough cookie."

Cole stood, reached out and took CJ's hand to help

her to her feet. He stopped himself from letting out an audible gasp as their hands met. Now that the unending anxiety was gone, her touch affected him even more profoundly than usual. What she'd made him feel before they'd been through a life-and-death struggle together had been bad enough. But now...

This was a disaster.

He could swear he felt an unbreakable connection forming between them the second their hands touched. As soon as she got to her feet, Cole let go and stepped back.

"Uh, Morning," he stammered. "She's trying to bear weight on that left hindquarter. Come see."

CJ blinked as if released from a trance and rushed forward. "Oh! She's better. Look how bright her eyes are," she cried.

Cole breathed a sigh of relief. They could focus their attention on Morning. He followed CJ and stood behind her as she caressed the mare's golden coat and murmured sweet words of praise. For the first time in years he got choked up seeing an owner with an ailing pet. This wasn't good at all.

CJ whirled toward him, a smile as bright as a summer's dawn lighting her face. "Thank you," she said, and threw her arms around his waist. "Thank you for not giving up on her. And especially for not letting me give up."

Cole wondered if his heart would ever start beating again. Then it did, and he worried that it might pound right out of his chest. If touching her hand had nearly short-circuited his nervous system, surely death would follow the pleasure of merely holding her close. And he *was* holding her, even though he'd made no conscious decision to return her embrace.

Then the mare whuffled and broke the spell CJ's nearness cast on him. Cole took her wrists to put her away from him. At least that was the plan. But when she looked at him with those tear-washed golden eyes, her lips so close to his, he lost his resolve. Who was he trying to kid? He lost his mind.

Closing the distance, Cole bent toward her, covering those tempting lips with his. And this time it was he who initiated the embrace. This time it was he who held on for dear life. This time he wished he never had to let go. As sweet as honey and as enthralling as the most authentic fantasy he'd ever envisioned, she held him captive with the honesty and innocence of her response.

He absorbed the feel of her in his arms for another day. He knew without a doubt that she was dangerous to his peace of mind, but he couldn't resist the urge to keep her right there in his arms where he could feel her heart beating so close to his. Where her lips had softened allowing him to deepen the kiss.

"Oh, dear. Excuse me." He heard Aunt Meg speak from a thousand miles away. CJ pulled back, breaking the connection between them, leaving Cole bereft and disoriented. Then undiluted reality dawned.

What had he done?

He managed to focus on CJ, who was as flustered

as he was, but who was at least trying to cover her nervousness with bright chatter.

"We were celebrating. Congratulating each other. Morning's better this morning." She looked adorable, flushed and embarrassed. She brushed off her jeans and smiled nervously. "Oh, that sounds so silly, doesn't it? My mother warned me her name was always going to sound redundant before noon, but what was I to do? She just looked like a Morning."

Chapter Nine

She was babbling, CJ realized. And Meg Taggert had the most annoyingly self-satisfied smirk on her face CJ had ever seen.

"Well, you're up and about early, Aunt Meg," Cole said, filling the silence CJ's sudden halt in run-on sentences had left.

"Dear boy, sleeping late with the furor you two have caused is a bit difficult."

"But we just..." Cole clearly was befuddled by the same thing that had CJ so nonplussed. He had only just kissed her. How could his family be upset already? Experience had taught her that families rarely approved of employees—and that was the way they all had to think of her—becoming personally involved with someone from their exclusive inner circle. They might invite her to dinner, but that was as far as they'd want the friendliness to go. Would this put her job in jeopardy? It had happened not so long ago.

Meg laughed and clapped her hands as if to get their attention. "Try to remember the rest of the world, you two. The horse? The virus? The media all but storming our gates?"

CJ tried to ignore how cute Cole had looked all flustered and confused. After a quick blink of his eyes that cleared them of their adorable fogginess, Cole said, "Morning just started showing improvement. We didn't have time to tell anyone."

Afraid Meg might mention that they'd had time to celebrate, CJ tried to head off any further comment on the kiss she'd interrupted. "Is there anything I can do for you?" she asked as Meg Taggert continued to stare expectantly at Cole.

Meg's penetrating gaze slid to CJ. "I do believe you already have," she murmured as she breezed past CJ to go into Morning's stall.

CJ just stared, then her gaze flew to Cole. She was relieved to see that he had not heard his aunt's comment. Considering the way Cole had reacted when CJ first arrived, when he thought that Hope might be playing matchmaker, CJ was thankful for small favors. The change in the relationship between them was too new, too special to come under the scrutiny and pressure of outsiders. She could see that he was anxious and unsure about it, too.

Before her parents were killed there had been a couple of boys she'd been infatuated with, but they had never returned her feelings. After that she'd been so busy keeping things at the farm together she'd had little time to even think about romance.

Before Cole, the only man who had ever paid attention to her was the son of the owner of the resort where she'd been in charge of the stables. His attentions had been unwanted, and CJ had been forced to physically discourage him when he'd kissed her against her will and had refused to let her go. Furious and insulted, he'd gone to his father and gotten her fired on the excuse that she'd been the one pressing for an unwanted relationship. When CJ had protested that it had been his unwanted advances that had caused the confrontation, her boss had not cared. She was beneath his son, no matter who was enamored of whom. She'd been given her walking papers almost immediately.

Meg barreled out of the stall and dragged CJ back to the present. Her hands on her hips, Meg considered the two of them. CJ was a little uncomfortable under her scrutiny, and it was clear Cole shared her feelings.

"Well, now, I can see I arrived just in time. You two are utterly exhausted. CJ, I want you to march yourself home and sleep. Now. And I don't mean take a nap. I mean get in bed and sleep till you wake up. Cole, I want you to give me any instructions for the care this animal needs for the rest of the day. And then you go up and get some sleep, too. If she needs anything that only you can provide, I'll wake you when the time comes."

"I don't feel comfortable with that. If you'll watch

her, I'll sack out on the couch in CJ's office. That way I'll be close if you need me."

Meg crossed her arms. "I'm sure that's not going to do it. You look like death warmed over, my boy. Your circles have circles. With that shoulder as sore as it must be, you need a bed not an old beat-up couch. CJ, get out of here and leave this stubborn ox to me. I'll see he takes care of himself, so you needn't worry."

CJ recognized futility even if Cole didn't. She nodded and left him to the tender mercies of his tyrannical aunt. It was perhaps the best way to thank the man who had saved her precious mare. The man CJ realized she was fast coming to love.

At her cottage, she did as ordered. She showered and minutes later slid between the sheets. But sleep was impossible with the memory of Cole's kiss and the feelings he evoked running through her. She remained stubbornly awake long into the afternoon. Then, when she finally did unwind enough to sleep, images of him made what sleep she got restless and troubled. Theirs had not been an easy acquaintance so far. How could love survive such diverse pasts and beliefs?

It was no wonder she didn't wake till the dawn of the new day. And after those first few moments of sleepy fog drifted away from her mind, the events of the day before sprang to the front of her thoughts once again.

Morning had passed the crisis, and Cole Taggert had kissed her, each event fulfilling every one of her impossible wishes. And more unbelievable, his aunt, at least, approved. None of it seemed possible. CJ felt like Cinderella arriving at the ball.

She jumped up and dressed quickly, anxiously anticipating what he would say to her now that he'd revealed his attraction to her. She had never even hoped he could feel that way toward her with Elizabeth Boyer in his life.

She wanted to see him, but there was a problem. If she saw him she needed to know how to act. Did she act cool and aloof? Interested only in Morning as if kisses like his happened to her every day? Or did she reveal how special he was to her and how unusual her attraction to him was?

Unsettled, CJ forced herself to go to the clinic. She expected to find Meg Taggert still standing guard. Instead, she found Cole engrossed in some sort of report.

"How's the patient?" she asked, hating the tentative tone in her voice.

Cole's head snapped up, and he jumped to his feet. "Go see. I think it's safe to say she's even stronger today. It'll take a while for the ataxia to clear up completely, but she's definitely on the road to recovery."

"That is such a relief," she said. "I was afraid she'd fail while I slept. Since no other horses have gotten sick, does that put Laurel Glen in the clear?"

Cole pinched the bridge of his nose and shook his head. "No. The incubation period is five to fifteen days, and there could be a lot more infected mosquitoes out there.''

So that was why he still looked so worried. "I'll keep my eye out for symptoms in the other animals then." She yawned, then let out a nervous chuckle. "I didn't sleep very well thinking about all that happened yesterday." Morning trumpeted a greeting. "Uh-oh, I'd better go say good day to our Morning."

She whirled away with more energy than she'd thought she'd have and went to visit with Morning. But her mind was filled with Cole. He looked tired and hadn't shaved. It gave him a rugged look she found just as attractive as the affable charmer he showed the rest of the world. He was really a combination of both, she supposed.

She left Morning and found Cole leaning against a steel table. He didn't look happy. His lips were pursed, and his arms, though one was still in sling, were crossed almost combatively. "CJ, we need to talk," he said.

CJ glanced at her mare. "Is it looking as if there's some permanent damage to Morning?"

"The subject is damage, but not to Morning. I'm concerned about damage to you."

"Your aunt Meg doesn't approve, after all."

"CJ there's nothing to approve of. There can't be. I really like you. Yesterday morning when I kissed you I was a little carried away by my relief and, quite frankly, Aunt Meg was right about my condition, I was exhausted. I don't want you to misinterpret what that was all about."

"Misinterpret?" she asked. Her voice sounded wooden. *I really like you.* Suddenly she felt as if the clock had struck midnight, ending her Cinderella fantasy.

"As I said, I like you," he continued. "A lot. But…" He took what she guessed would be considered a fortifying breath. It hurt that talking to her was suddenly so difficult for him. "CJ, you're not the kind of woman who goes around kissing men without your emotions getting involved. I know that about you. What I don't think you know about me is that I can. I have no choice. I just don't *do* love. The whole idea of forever is a concept I can't wrap my mind around. Elizabeth and I…we're, ah, close. She doesn't mind a limited relationship."

CJ would never know where the strength to bluff her way out of there came from, but she had a good idea, and she'd thank Him later. She smiled and thought she pulled it off rather well.

"You've gotten yourself all upset over nothing. I understood. We were celebrating, just as I told your aunt. You know how important my faith is to me, Cole. I couldn't become involved that way with someone who doesn't share my beliefs no matter how attractive I find him. Besides which, I've seen Elizabeth. Why would you even look my way with someone like her on your arm?"

"No," he protested. "It's me, not you."

CJ arched her eyebrow in disbelief. "I'm clearly not your type, nor would I want to be. As you say, that just isn't me." She checked her watch. "I'm glad we got this settled. I'd love to stay and chat but I'm late for daily briefing. Should I ask Jack to assign someone to watch Morning?''

Cole frowned and then nodded.

Having granted his reprieve, CJ turned and fled, praying she'd get out of the barn and to relative privacy before she burst into tears. What a fool she'd been! Why would Prince Charming want a Cinderella who wore manure-stained boots to the ball when he already had a princess on his arm with a closet full of glass slippers?

Cole felt about as low as a man could. He'd hurt her. She'd put up a good front, but not a good enough one to hide her pain from an expert. How many times had he played this scene, and with women better equipped to handle rejection than CJ? Did she think he was so shallow as to prefer Elizabeth because she'd been ruthlessly polished into a model debutante by parents for whom appearance was everything? And did she think she was somehow beneath his notice because she didn't choose to kowtow at the throne of fashion? Apparently she did.

But he wouldn't change what he'd done even to restore her good opinion of him. He'd done what he had to do. She was not the kind of woman to kiss a man the way she had and not have her heart involved. And her heart had been in that kiss, no matter what nonsense she'd blathered on about concerning his lack of faith. If what they'd shared was a celebration, it was not about her horse but because she'd thought her feelings for him were reciprocated.

He couldn't deny that they were. He *did* care for her. Too much. But he also knew that sooner or later he'd panic and pull back. Better to hurt her a little while she still had her dignity and privacy. If he'd waited, hadn't stopped this now, more people than Aunt Meg would have realized how CJ felt about him. Then when he broke it off, she would no doubt have felt the need to leave Laurel Glen.

He'd thought long and hard and far into the night, and he couldn't take a chance on that happening. He would leave before letting her go out in the world alone again. At least if she was at Laurel Glen, he'd know she was safe and happy.

"Cole," Hope called on her way down the hall from the offices. "Oh, good. You *are* here. I just saw CJ running to her cottage. She looked upset, as if she might be crying. Is Morning worse again?"

Cole's heart plummeted. He'd made her cry. That wasn't what he'd wanted. It was what he'd hoped to avoid. He wanted to comfort her, but that would only negate the benefits of what he'd done. And he couldn't send Hope to comfort her. CJ would be mortified to learn he'd been talking about their kiss to anyone. Best to stay the course, even though he wanted to cry, too.

"She was emotional about the mare. She said she didn't sleep very well, so that's probably why."

"Oh, well, I just saw Elizabeth driving in. I thought I'd warn you."

"Warn me?"

"Aunt Meg mentioned that, ah, you and CJ were—"

"Well, Aunt Meg's jumping to conclusions. What she saw was just a friendly kiss. It didn't mean a thing other than that we were happy the mare had rallied."

Hope's gaze went stormy. "It didn't mean anything to *you,* you mean! CJ left here crying over you and this attitude of yours, didn't she? Obviously a kiss means a lot more to her than to you. Really, Cole, how could you toy with someone as inexperienced as CJ Larson? She isn't in Elizabeth's league, and you know it!"

"And how, Hope dear, would you know what *league* I'm in?"

"Play in the mud, Elizabeth, and you get it all over yourself," Hope said, and turned to glare at Elizabeth. She followed his friend with her angry gaze as Elizabeth walked to stand next to him. "It's really quite easy to spot," she continued, then pinned him with that same look of ire. "I'll go see if I can calm CJ down."

"Leave CJ alone!" Cole snapped. "If she thinks anyone knows what went on between us, she'll bolt. Do you want her out there somewhere, homeless again, in that rattletrap of a truck? Do you want her leaving that mare behind to avoid embarrassment?"

"No, we wouldn't want that, would we?" Hope said with that supercilious left eyebrow of hers arched, then after looking from him to Elizabeth and back again, she sent him a bratty smirk and left.

Cole shuddered at the thought of the damage she could wreak in his life and in CJ's. "Save the world from obnoxious little sisters," he grumbled.

"Mind telling me what I did to get on Hope's wrong side? *Again?*" Elizabeth asked. He understood her emphasis. Elizabeth had shown up at a charity dance with Jeff a year and a half ago and had caused a ripple on the sea of romance for Jeff and Hope. Hope had invited him to attend the Valentine's Day dance as her date, but Jeff had been blind to the woman Hope had become. He'd misunderstood the invitation and had arrived as Elizabeth's escort.

"It's my fault," Cole admitted. "And I'm sorry. I've been using you, and I just did it again. Not only didn't I ask you for permission, but now I have to ask you to continue the charade."

"Used me how, and what charade?"

Cole grimaced. This wouldn't be easy. "My family just assumes we're, well, you know—involved. And I've just let them go on assuming."

Elizabeth sat heavily on the desk chair next to him. "Oh, Cole, how could you? I trusted you to be my friend."

"I *am* your friend. Have I ever told a single soul you were with me that night in the police car? Have I even admitted anyone was with me? I just didn't see any harm in not continuing to deny a relationship when they wouldn't believe me, anyway."

"But that's why they all act as if they don't approve of me."

"You don't know that. You're different from Hope, so she isn't comfortable with you. And Aunt Meg just doesn't think we suit each other, and we've both agreed that's true. Right? You do still feel only friendship toward me?"

"Don't get that worried look. You aren't about to break my heart." Her pretty green eyes widened. "Oh. But you have broken that nice CJ Larson's heart, and you used me as an excuse to do it. Right?"

"I didn't mean to."

"Oh? Someone else put the words your mouth? A fairy snuck in here and cast a spell on you?"

"I *did* mean to use our relationship. I *didn't* mean to hurt her," he clarified. "At least not badly. I knew telling her the two of us are involved would hurt her, but I thought it was necessary. I also didn't mean for her to care for me. And I sure didn't mean to kiss her."

"It seems there's been a lot of things going on around here that you didn't mean. Did you by any chance not mean to fall in love with her?"

"I don't love her," he denied a little too vehemently. "You know that. I can't. If I tried, I'd fail, and then she'd be hurt much more than ending it now. I'm afraid she'd leave." Even the thought of her out there alone gave him a desolate feeling. "She has no one, Elizabeth. She's lost everyone. Her father. Her mother. Her grandfather. Even her home. If she left here, she'd have nowhere to go. At least this way I can watch out for her, make sure she's okay.''

Elizabeth gave him one of her long, hard stares then sighed. ''Oh, all right. I could never say no to you. What do you want me to do?''

''Nothing. Not really. Just hang out with me the way we do already. You come to dinner. We go out to dinner. We go riding.''

''Fine. But just for the record, I think it's too late. From Hope's reaction just now, I'd say she thinks it's too late for CJ. And I think you care more about CJ than you want to admit.''

It wasn't that he didn't want to admit it. He couldn't. He just *couldn't.*

Chapter Ten

Cole didn't see CJ for the rest of the day. Hope hadn't gone to offer comfort, either; she'd decided that he might be right about CJ being embarrassed by her feelings for him.

He'd gone for a ride to clear his head and give Mischief some much-needed exercise. He reined in the gelding and sat atop a hill trying to find some peace as he looked over Laurel Glen's front entrance arch. The laurel was still in full bloom—a riot of color against a backdrop of varying shades of green.

He imagined that his parents, grandparents and great-grandparents before him had sat on horseback contemplating the same quiet scene. Things were getting back to normal at Laurel Glen after the disasters of the summer before. Peace had returned, even though the business still had some important ground to regain. His father had done it before. He'd do it again.

What was it that gave Ross the confidence to forge ahead with adversity all around him? Could it be this faith of his?

CJ said it was so important to her she wouldn't have considered a relationship with him, even if he'd wanted one, unless he was willing to embrace her faith. He still believed she'd already come to care for him, but what she'd said about her faith was the one part of her little speech that rang true. And that bothered him.

Talk about a dog in the manger.

He knew he should be glad she had already seen impediments to a relationship between them. And he was.

But her reason bothered him. It didn't seem fair. He had every right to be angry at God. Granny Taggert had spent years telling him how much God loved all His creatures. How, if Cole would just believe in Him, God would protect him. And he'd begun to believe it all. Yet at the moment of his greatest need, God had turned His back on Cole. God had let that spawn-of-the-devil stallion kill Cole's mother. He'd sat up in heaven watching as Cole had watched while Marley Taggert was trampled to death. God had ignored the anguished cries of woman and boy.

Cole was willing to admit to the existence of God, but he could not believe God took any control over events on earth. If He did, Cole could not see how God could be just, kind or good. And so Cole had turned his back on the God who'd stood by and watched as Cole's world was destroyed.

"I'd offer a penny for your thoughts, but it looks to me as if they're worth at least a dollar."

Cole started at the sound of his aunt's voice, causing Mischief to dance nervously sideways. He got the gelding under control then turned toward Meg. "Sorry, I didn't hear you."

"So are you going to pass up that dollar?" Aunt Meg asked with a gentle smile.

"Just thinking about the past, the present and future."

"My, that's some ambitious thinking you're up to. And what conclusion have you come to?"

"That I'll never understand any of it." He rubbed his forehead and forced a little chuckle. "That thinking too much just gives me a headache."

"This does sound serious. Trouble in paradise? I was surprised to see Elizabeth here."

Cole knew a fishing expedition when he heard one. And having obtained Elizabeth's permission to use her shamelessly as a smoke screen, he quickly formulated an appropriate answer. "She stopped at a car wash before coming so she wouldn't have to worry about bringing any of Reginald's contaminated mosquitoes with her. She's afraid that's what happened. I don't blame either of them for what happened. I can't. It was a chance occurrence. Elizabeth still feels terrible about Morning. I'm hoping none of the family takes it out on her. I'm sure CJ wouldn't want that to happen."

"What about CJ and Elizabeth?"

"One has nothing to do with the other. CJ is my friend, and Elizabeth… Well, Elizabeth is—"

Meg cleared her throat. "I know, dear boy, what Elizabeth is. When I saw you and CJ in each other's arms yesterday, I'd hoped you'd realized it, too. I don't mind telling you how disappointed I am with you that you would play around with such a sweet young woman's heart. CJ deserves better."

"Did it ever occur to you that it's CJ who finds me unworthy? For heaven's sake, Aunt Meg, we have nothing in common but our love of animals. She isn't anything like the women I date, and I don't share her faith, which makes me not good enough for her."

Aunt Meg looked terribly sad. "You know, dear, I've always loved you like a son, and I only want what's best for you. I think CJ could be very good for you, but I won't push, since the two of you seem to have come to a parting of ways. Now we'd better get a move on before we're late for dinner."

Meg wheeled her mount away from him and cast him a sly look. "Last one to the stable rubs down both animals." With that, she took off downhill, riding like a woman half her age and leaving him to bring up the rear. It was, of course, a no-win situation for Cole. He'd never let his aunt do his work for him, and she would never welsh on a bet. So he had no choice but to let her win the impromptu race.

Laughing, he followed her into the yard and jumped down off Mischief. "You cheated," he accused.

She shot him a crooked, mischievous smile. "That's the prerogative of age, darling boy."

"Shall I have a couple of men take care of your horses?" Jack Alton asked as he walked out of one of the stables and into the yard.

Aunt Meg turned quickly and stared at Alton. She said nothing for a long moment. Then she blinked. Cole figured the foreman's appearance was enough to give any family member pause.

"And who would this young man be?" she asked.

"Oh, I'm sorry, Aunt Meg," Cole said. "This is Jack Alton. He's the guy Dad hired to take Donovan's place. Jack, this is my aunt Meg. Surrogate mother to all of Laurel Glen."

Alton narrowed his eyes a bit. "Would that make you Meg Taggert?"

"Well, yes, it would."

"Ma'am, this may sound like a foolish question, but were you in *Hello, Dolly* on Broadway in the sixties? I think I remember your name from a playbill my parents brought home from a trip to New York. It was before my time, but as a kid I always got a kick out of looking at all the things they saved from their marriage."

"Actually, yes, I was in *Hello, Dolly.* I was in the chorus." Meg frowned. "Where did you say you're from?"

"Out west ma'am. I'd already talked to your brother about the job here so your name stuck in my head when I saw the playbill. It's a small world, they say. So, Cole, do you want me to have one of the men see to your animals?''

Cole nearly said yes, but Aunt Meg shot him a look that said he'd lost the race square if not fair. He sighed. While that was debatable, he didn't want to press the issue. "I'll take care of them. A bet is a bet, and she beat me even if she cheated."

Meg raised her eyebrow. Her lips tipped up, and she put her hands on her slim hips. "I've never cheated at anything in my life!" she declared with a sly grin.

His aunt had the figure of a woman half her age. She was young-looking if you ignored her white hair. And she was pretty, too. He never understood why men weren't lining up down Laurel Glen's drive in the hopes of replacing her long-ago love.

"Hurry now," Meg added. "Ruth Ann will have your head if you're late for dinner, and I'm not getting between the two of you again. Besides, it's been days since you had a meal with the family."

"It'll just be the family this time. Right?"

"CJ isn't invited, if that's what you mean. I promise you I won't push. That would just hurt both of you. But don't expect me never to invite her. She's part of Laurel Glen now, and we all like her."

He liked her, too. Too much!

CJ looked around the yard before stepping out of Stable Two. She'd somehow managed to avoid Cole all day Thursday and Friday and for the entire weekend. The Fourth of July holiday on Friday had helped because the family had local Independence Day observances and an impressive list of private celebrations to attend.

She'd noticed Mischief was out of his stall and that Cole was nowhere in sight. He usually rode Mischief in the early evenings and came back at about dusk, so finding his gelding gone before the dinner hour was unusual.

"He rode south about an hour and a half ago. I'd say you're safe for a while, anyway," Jack Alton told her with too much sympathy in his voice for CJ's comfort.

"Who rode south?" CJ asked, playing dumb and hoping the bright sunshine would hide her discomfort. It was clear that Jack was on to her. And she knew why. He looked so much like Cole that a couple of times she'd started to head in the other direction when she saw him then quickly changed direction again when she realized who it was. She was sure he'd noticed.

"CJ, I'd like to think we've at least developed a nice friendly working relationship since I started here."

"So would I."

"Look, I don't want to intrude, but you can't keep tiptoeing around here like some sort of timid spirit. I don't know what happened between you and Cole Taggert while Morning was so critical but something clearly did. Would it help to talk about it?"

CJ shook her head. "I'm fine really. What could possibly have happened? He has Elizabeth in his life and I'm..." She looked down at herself and chuckled. It had rained heavily overnight, and the lower paddocks were mud holes. A lot of that mud had splashed all over her when Demon got playful during his training session.

Jack shook his head and jammed his hands in his back pockets. "If Cole Taggert is stupid enough to prefer a lazy dilettante like Elizabeth Boyer, he deserves what he gets."

CJ blinked and stepped back from Jack. He was about the most mild-mannered man she'd ever met, so why was he so against Elizabeth, who was one of the nicest women CJ had ever dealt with?

"I think you're being more than a little hard on her. Elizabeth's really quite nice. It isn't as if she asked to be born into a socially prominent family. Besides, I didn't know you'd spent enough time with her in the week and a half you've been here to let you form an opinion of her character."

"I didn't need much time at all. She's come here to ride and hasn't once offered to saddle or unsaddle the horse she rides. Nor has she ever offered to rub him down. Then, when I asked her if she'd made sure no mosquitoes had ridden in on her car, she just glared at me and stalked off. I was only trying to point out how careful she should be considering where the infestation was found."

"Jack, she's had her car washed every time she's come here. And did you ever consider that she doesn't offer to help with the horses because she's been taught that she shouldn't? It isn't right to judge someone so rashly."

Jack Alton sighed and nodded, then looked at the ground. He frowned, clearly troubled. "You're right. I know you're right. I guess it's just habit. A bad habit. It's something I struggle with."

"Have you had time to check out the church the Taggerts attend?" CJ asked.

"No, I hadn't thought to ask anyone. The first Sunday I was here Morning had come down with West Nile so I was pretty snowed under. And yesterday I wandered into the little old church out on the main drag. It was okay but not very inspiring."

"You might like the Tabernacle. The pastor is a wonderful man, and so is the rest of the congregation. It's a big church, but it never feels big."

"Thanks for the tip. I'll give it a try," Jack promised. "And here's a tip for you. You need to get away from here for a little while. I have to take a drive up to the King of Prussia area. They have a huge movie house up there. I'm not sure what's playing, but there has to be something worth seeing with ten theaters. I think it would do you a world of good to be shut of this place for the evening. Want to ride along?"

CJ wasn't sure. Jack was nice and every bit as handsome as Cole, but he wasn't Cole. Cole had her heart, and she didn't know how to get it back. "I don't know, Jack."

Jack smiled. "Relax. I didn't mean this would be

a date. We'll just be two friends seeing a movie to-gether.''

CJ didn't miss the irony that she wasn't at all upset by Jack's request they be just friends, yet when Cole said the same thing she had been devastated. Why couldn't she have waited and fallen in love with Jack Alton?

''I'd love to see a movie, and I'd like very much for us to be friends. I was in King of Prussia once, and they have a food court at one of the malls. Suppose I get cleaned up and we eat there, too.''

Cole came over the hill at a fast canter. Amelia, CJ and Jack Alton stood talking near Alton's pickup where it was parked in the drive near the yard. They all turned and looked as he brought Mischief into a trot and wheeled toward the practice ring. He'd just dismounted when Amelia broke away with a friendly wave and headed toward him. Trying to ignore CJ and Alton, Cole studiously watched his stepmother move toward him.

But as if his eyes had minds of their own, his gaze shifted to CJ as she climbed into Alton's shining teal pickup and remained on her until they drove away. He continued to watch as the pickup wended its way down the drive.

''Why so annoyed?'' Amelia asked when she reached him.

''I'm not annoyed. I just don't trust that guy. I'm telling you, it's just plain creepy how much he looks like pictures of Granddad. I can't believe it's coincidence. I'm going to give Jim Lovell a call. Maybe he can find out something about Jack Alton of the Circle A, Torrence, Colorado.''

"Ross checked him out. Just because Jack used neighbors and not his father for his references is no reason to suspect the man has anything to hide. He admitted he isn't getting along with his father right now. You more than anyone else should understand and sympathize with someone who has a rocky relationship with his father. I think you're just jealous.''

Cole stared at Amelia. Could that be it? As he'd watched the pickup disappear from sight his chest had felt hollow and his stomach had tightened as if he were angry. But he'd had no reason to feel angry. Still, there was no denying that he had been and still was angry. He *must* be jealous.

And that wasn't good, especially if Amelia could see it. He had no say, nor should he want a say in what CJ did. He'd told her in no uncertain terms that those were rights he didn't want. And he didn't. He couldn't. Now if he could only convince himself.

"I have no reason to be jealous of Alton and CJ,'' Cole replied, instead of admitting the truth. He tried to look unaffected and too superior to fall prey to so base an emotion as envy.

Amelia stared at him. He was braced for her to go into her steel magnolia mode, but she threw him a curve. She was all soft and round in her advanced state of pregnancy, and a profound disappointment and sadness descended on her features. It nearly killed him to be the cause, then she added the death blow.

"I thought we were friends," she said, her blue-gray eyes suddenly misty and suspicious at once.

"We *are* friends."

"Friends don't lie to each other, Cole."

"CJ's all alone in the world. I just worry about her," he defended, trying to throw suspicion elsewhere. "There's nothing deep and hidden about it. I'm worried about all of us. I can't believe Dad isn't. He hasn't even mentioned Alton's resemblance to Granddad."

"Perhaps that's because he knew your grandfather, and you didn't. He *has* recognized the resemblance but just as quickly dismissed it as coincidence. He says his father would never have allowed one of his sons to be raised away from Laurel Glen. For your father, his belief in the man who raised him is enough.

"Now, on the subject of CJ, it wasn't her date with Jack Alton that I was referring to. I thought perhaps you were jealous of how well Jack and your father get along." She shot him gleeful little grin. "But now that you mention it, you and CJ would make nice couple. Funny, I hadn't thought of her as your type. Want to talk about it?"

In an uncharacteristic moment of openness, Cole nodded. For most of his adult life he'd been alone with no one to confide in. That had been a mistake. He'd kept everyone who came into his life at arm's length. The purpose of his return home was to correct that character flaw. A therapist he'd seen in California felt that his separation from his family—Ross in particular—was at the root of his problems with his relationships.

"I know I have no right to ask you to keep secrets from my father, but I do need someone talk to. I'm just not sure I can be completely honest if I think the minute you leave here you're going to go right to him with everything I say."

"No, you don't have that right. But unless something you tell me affects him, my relationship with him or the farm, I see no reason to approach him with information he doesn't need. To me that would feel like gossiping."

Once again Cole found himself nodding. She clearly didn't believe he had no interest beyond friendship with CJ. And he did need a sounding board. "I do care about CJ, but I told her we could only be friends. I told her Elizabeth was the reason."

"Why would you do that? I don't understand you. If you care this much about CJ, why are you still carrying on with Elizabeth Boyer?"

Cole shook his head. He'd really dug a hole where Elizabeth was concerned. He stayed silent for a long moment as he watched the plume of dust kicked up by the pickup finally settle. Then he took a deep breath. Time to face the music. "Because, first of all, I'm not carrying on with Elizabeth at all. I tried to tell everyone in the beginning she was just a friend, but no one would believe me. I got sick of trying so I let it ride. And, truthfully, that suited me just fine.

It kept Hope and Aunt Meg from playing matchmaker.

"As for why I told CJ we can only be friends..." Cole paused and sighed. "I don't want to hurt her. She's not as experienced as the other women I've tried to have relationships with, and I've hurt them. I *will* hurt CJ if I let her go on caring for me. I thought it would be better to cut off whatever this is between us right now. If I'd just told her I can't seem to love anyone, she would have thought, just as some other women have, that she might be the one person I could love. And when I couldn't—" He shook his head. "No. I just couldn't do that to her. So I told her Elizabeth and I are involved."

Amelia, heavy with child, sank down on a hay bale. "Who are you really trying to protect? CJ or you? What truly stopped you with those other women you mentioned?"

Cole stared at Amelia. The shrink in California had only been partly right. Lately he'd begun to wonder if there wasn't more. The fear had only become worse since he learned of his mother's betrayal with Donovan. "Me, I'm afraid. I think of getting hurt the way Mom must have hurt Dad," he admitted before he could chicken out. He had never admitted it aloud to anyone. He'd barely faced it himself.

"Don't you think that someone like CJ—someone with such a good heart—would be just the kind of person you need? Maybe, instead of hiding from her, you should seek her out."

Cole dropped down next to Amelia. He could have

sworn he'd gone all light-headed at her suggestion. He couldn't risk it. "I don't think so. The whole point was not to hurt her any more than I already have."

"I'm not talking about a love affair, and you know it. That sort of thing is wrong with a capital W and would devastate someone of CJ's deep faith. I'm talking about real committed love. I'm talking about learning to trust a woman with your heart—not just your friendship."

Chapter Eleven

Cole entered the breakfast room the next morning with his mind still on his conversation with Amelia. Aunt Meg was there, as were his father and Amelia. Ross looked up, and Cole held his breath. Had Amelia told Ross or kept Cole's confidence? He wasn't sure what he wanted her to have done.

"Oh, good, son, you're still here," his father said. "I was hoping to run into you before you left for your first call. I have a couple of geldings coming in today. Swedish warm bloods. Can you be on hand when they arrive?"

It was in Cole's contract as Laurel Glen's vet that he was to check out every animal arriving at the farm regardless of where they had last been stabled. After Cole nodded his agreement, Ross went on to give him a rundown of the horses and their owners.

"Got any idea what time they'll arrive?" Cole asked, then let out a pent-up breath. His father certainly didn't act any different. Maybe Amelia hadn't said anything about their talk.

Ross shook his head. "I'm not sure. Check with CJ. She took the last call about the transfer."

Cole stared at his father. Was this an attempt to throw them together? He had no way of knowing, and that left him with a dilemma. So soon after his talk with Amelia, he still hadn't decided if he'd follow her advice. Deciding to take the low road and put off a face-to-face encounter with CJ for as long as possible, he waited until he got to the office to call her and check on the arrival time of the geldings.

All day, whenever his mind wasn't occupied with his patients, Cole went over and over all the things Amelia had said the night before. He could come to no other conclusion but that she was right. He couldn't continue to run from confronting his problems. The only answer was to see if his undeniable attraction to—okay, near obsession with—CJ could be nurtured into something more. Maybe it *was* time he learned to give his heart. And who else better to give it to than CJ, someone who was so worthy of his trust?

Still, he couldn't let her know his true relationship with Elizabeth. It was the best way he knew to protect her from hoping too much for a future with him. With the warning that he only wanted friendship already in place, it was less likely he would break her heart if he couldn't come to love and trust her enough to form a foundation on which they could build a future together.

The only worry he had left with regard to CJ was that she seemed to consider him no better than a heathen and might not be willing to give him a chance at all. He knew it was his fault for overreacting to his attraction to her and for the way he had chosen to discourage it. He'd been an idiot.

As he approached the stables, Cole grew apprehensive. CJ walked into the sunlight, and he knew he had to try. Striving for a light, friendly approach, he tooted his horn as he pulled to a stop in the drive.

"Have the new boys arrived?" he called, hoping she wouldn't stalk off in the other direction.

She smiled and waved instead, and Cole breathed a relieved sigh. She didn't hate him. That was a start.

"They only just arrived," she shouted in answer as she walked toward him. "The poor babies had such a long trip from their last facility I decided to turn them out into the practice ring so they could run off a little steam," she continued when she reached the fence of the practice ring.

Cole nodded and climbed out of his SUV. Then CJ turned to leave. "Could you hang around so I can give you a verbal report?" he asked. "I have a mare in labor at Flushing Green and I want to get back as soon as possible."

He didn't wait for an answer but approached the practice ring, trying to ignore the effect CJ had on him now that he'd held her close and kissed her. It was even more profound than before. He hoped he wasn't already in over his head.

Forcing his attention to the newest residents of

Laurel Glen, Cole considered the two newcomers with a critical eye. They both had the good lines consistent with their breed. One was a rich, warm brown with a wide, white blaze and stockings and a darker brown mane and tail. The other was a deeper brown with no markings at all and a mane and tail that matched his coat. Both geldings looked to stand about sixteen hands high, and both seemed to have decent form and dispositions.

"You don't often see beauties like these. They keep the best to stand at stud and work in major competitions," he said as he leaned on the top rail. "It was the owner's good luck these two are a little on the small side."

For a long moment CJ looked at the tall trees and the beautiful green fields that surrounded them as she studiously ignored the tall, beautiful man next to her. Then she inhaled a deep breath and put her trust in the Lord. He would have to protect her heart because it was vulnerable to Cole, and she didn't seem to be able to do a thing about it.

"When I see perfection like these two and all this beauty around us, I know there's a grand design to the world," she told Cole. "I'll never understand how people can think this is all an accident."

Cole's smile was a little sad. "I'm not a heathen, CJ."

"I never said you were. At least I never meant to," she protested, in a mild state of shock that her comment hadn't annoyed him in the least.

In fact, she didn't remember ever seeing Cole so content. She didn't know what had changed, but for the first time he wasn't looking for a way to start an argument with her. The only explanation was that he'd employed verbal sparring to keep her at arm's length, and now that he had explained his relationship with Elizabeth, he must be sure she would see him as just a friend. Unfortunately, CJ was sure that was impossible.

"You as much as called me a heathen the other day," he surprised her by saying. "Of course, it's probably my fault. I came on a little strong about my objections to God and religion when we first met, but I never said I don't believe He exists. I just don't believe I can put my trust in Him. There's a big difference. Why pray to Someone who can't or won't help when you need Him?"

CJ wasn't sure whether to debate this with him or not, but he did bring up the subject. "Pastor Jim would say that's a vending machine attitude toward prayer and God."

"How's that?"

"Well, when you step up to a vending machine you stick money in and punch a button for what you want. Where's the difference between that and yelling out a prayer and expecting God to just hand you what you've asked for? You know, there are other answers to a request besides yes. Sometimes the answer is yes, sometimes it's wait, and sometimes it's just plain no."

She held her breath, waiting for an explosion, but

he merely nodded and said, "I can understand the answer might be no if someone is asking for a bicycle, a new car or even a job. But I was praying about life and death. I was desperate. Why would a just God let Mom die so young? So horribly?"

"Have you ever thought of all the other people out there who lose loved ones every day? People who call out in desperation for Him to save just this one person? Death is a part of life, as is tragedy. Do you think He doesn't feel or understand our pain? Remember, He had to watch while His Son was beaten, crowned with thorns then hung on a cross to die. He doesn't ask us to endure anything that He hasn't been through."

"Then why doesn't He want to spare us that pain?"

"What makes you think He doesn't want to? But if He did, He would be removing our free will, since death often occurs because of the exercise of free will."

Cole sighed. "I've heard that one before. Mom didn't have to get on Dynamite. The guy who sold him to Dad didn't have to be dishonest about previous problems. But none of that changes what happened."

"Look, Cole, Hope and I have become friends. I don't want you to think that we've been gossiping, but she's talked to me about your mother's death and the events that led up to it. You say you believe in God. Do you also believe He can see the future?"

Again, Cole didn't come back with an immediate

answer but thought for moment. "I suppose I do. What are you getting at?"

CJ shrugged. Even she wasn't sure yet. She often thought aloud, working out problems audibly. "I guess what I mean is God knows how the lives of His people will eventually turn out after they lose a loved one. Also, He knows that the other side of death can be heaven. It must have less of a sting for Him because of that."

"So, because the rest of us are doing all right, it was okay to let my mother be trampled to death?" His incredulous tone told CJ she was losing him with her partially formed logic.

"Just follow me here. Do you think it would be better for all of us to live our lives knowing the exact moment our deaths will come?"

Cole's mouth kicked up in a nervous grin. "Why do I feel as if that question is going to lead me into some sort of theological trap?"

CJ smiled back. She didn't care why Cole was suddenly so receptive. If it took facing the fact that he was way out of her league, then it was a price she was willing to pay. His eternity was a lot more important than her temporal happiness. She wasn't about to reject a chance to help Cole understand a few of the mysteries of life that she had been lucky enough to be taught early on when belief comes with childlike trust. She cared about him too much to be that selfish.

"Try to see this from a believer's point of view," she advised. "Christians believe that anyone who believes Jesus was the Son of God and who turns to Him as Savior with a repentant heart will go to heaven, even if they only turned to him in the last seconds of life. Maybe in those last horrible seconds your mother heard you calling out in the name of the Lord. Suppose she called out to Him as Lord and Savior.''

"Mom was pretty much against religion."

"She lived in a house with your great-grandmother and your grandfather. I've heard they were staunch believers. She had to have heard some of the Gospel. And when she started seeing your father, he was a churchgoer. He must have talked to her about the Lord, as well, which all means she'd heard about Him no matter how she was raised and what she said she believed.''

"And your point is?"

"There's an old saying, 'There are no atheists in foxholes.' She must've been very frightened during the attack and she had to know how much danger she was in. And she probably heard you calling on the Lord, reminding her that He was out there with His hand out to her.

"Suppose we agree that we only have so many days on earth and each person's number is different," she continued. "So that means it was her time to die no matter how it happened. Now suppose she'd simply died in her sleep or in a sudden fall or any way that gave her no warning of imminent death. It might have been less traumatic for those she left behind but that wouldn't have given her time to call on Him."

"So you're saying that to God, my mother's eternity might have been more important than how much her death adversely affected our lives or how frightening it was for her at the time."

CJ smiled. "Exactly. He sees death differently than we do because He sees the eternal side."

"But it's all speculation. According to your beliefs, if she didn't call out to Him, then she went to hell."

"And that is where an often misused quote from Matthew comes in. It's the beginning of the seventh chapter. 'Judge not that you be not judged.'"

Cole nodded. "I've heard that one. How could it be misused? It says it's wrong to say someone else is doing the wrong thing. That's one of my biggest complaints against religious people. They're always saying one thing or another is a sin. They try to make everyone else live according to their rules."

"That is exactly what I mean. You just misused it. It's a Christian's charge to be God's light in this world. Why is it that when someone who says they don't believe in God or religion hears their behavior called a sin against God—the God they say they don't believe in—they get all huffy? If they don't believe in Him, and they don't think they're doing anything wrong, why do they care what someone else thinks?"

Cole frowned and looked troubled. "I guess they're insulted in some way to be told they're wrong. Nobody likes to have a mirror held up to their lives and to find themselves lacking. So what do you think the quote means?''

''I think Jesus meant that it's no one's job but the Father's to pronounce heaven or hell on anyone's soul. That's God the Father's privilege alone, because only He knows what is in the heart of a person. The full quote is, 'Judge not, that you be not judged. For with what judgment you judge, you will be judged; and the measure you use, it will be measured back to you.' He means to be careful not to become judgmental, as in daring to judge someone else's motives, because our sins will be judged as harshly as we've judged others.''

''I never thought of it like that.'' His forehead creased in deep thought, he added, ''You've given me a lot to think about.''

CJ decided she couldn't ask for more than that, so she started asking him questions about the Swedish warm bloods.

Cole performed his usual magic on the two geldings and in minutes had the restive animals practically standing in line to do his bidding. She'd never seen anything like Cole in action. CJ was starting to think of him as the Dr. Dolittle of the equine world. The image made her smile.

When Cole arrived home late that afternoon, he went to the stables to meet Elizabeth. When he got to the stables—the center of all Laurel Glen's activities—he saw CJ putting Mischief through his paces at the end of a lunging line. It was amazing how much she'd done for the undisciplined animal he'd brought home to Laurel Glen over a year ago.

It was also amazing to him that someone who looked as delicate as she did could have the strength and stamina to work at the pace she did. She'd been on the job since just after dawn, and she still looked as if she could take on the world.

But the most amazing thing of all was that even from yards away, he could see the strength of character and determination that was at the core of her and present in every fiber of her being. She held Mischief to a trot with the force of her will alone. She'd lived a tough life and had never complained about the obstacles and tragedies she'd had to overcome. They had honed her solid, resolute spirit.

CJ had been only two or three years older than he was when his mother died, and she'd lost both her parents just as tragically. Then, after spending the next years trying desperately to hold on to her family's farm, she'd lost her grandfather and then the farm. It made him more than a little ashamed to have caved in under much less of a test.

A head butt from Mischief brought Cole out of his black study and back to the beautiful sunny afternoon. He regained his balance and automatically reached for Mischief's bridle. "How's my boy this afternoon?"

"He's a good boy," CJ crooned to the gelding as she stroked his velvety muzzle.

At the same time Cole ran his hand down Mischief's forehead, and his hand covered hers. They both froze, and their gazes locked. The only thing that released them was what sounded like a strident discussion in the yard near Stable Two. The spell broken, they turned in unison.

Jack Alton stood next to Elizabeth's little sports car. He wore the black Stetson he'd arrived in, but his body language was different. Gone were the laid-back country manners. In their place was a hostile stance.

Of course, the unflappable Elizabeth Boyer seemed just as furious when she dived into her car, revved the engine and took off down the drive at much too quick a pace for the low-slung little car on so bumpy a road.

"Now what do you suppose that was all about?" Cole asked rhetorically, certainly not expecting an answer.

"I imagine it was Jack's fault. For some weird reason Elizabeth makes him very annoyed. And from the way she just flew down the drive I would say he has the same effect on her. Weird. They're both such nice people." CJ looked at him in surprise. "Oh, I suppose she was here to go riding with you again. I'm sorry you lost your companion for the afternoon."

While he was concerned about what he'd witnessed, Elizabeth's departure didn't upset him as much as it made him curious. It also presented him with an opportunity.

"It does appear that way, doesn't it?" he said.

"Would you be able to ride with me? It's too beautiful a day to waste all on work."

It was clear he'd taken her by surprise. Cole didn't know what was rounder, CJ's big brown eyes or her mouth when she said, "Oh…you want *me* to go with you?"

"Are you too busy?" he asked and tried to ignore the twinge of sadness her incredulous attitude caused in the region of his heart.

She shook her head. "No, working with Mischief was the last thing I planned on doing today. It's just that I didn't think you wanted me around."

Later, he told himself, when he was sure he could be all she needed him to be, he'd make sure she understood why he'd pushed her away. He wanted her with him all the time, and it scared him silly. "Now where would you get a crazy idea like that? Have you ever ridden Queen Morgana?"

Chapter Twelve

There was a place on Laurel Glen that Cole loved more than any other. As often as he and Elizabeth rode, he'd never taken her there. In fact, he'd steered them in another direction whenever they approached this place because theirs was a friendship of the present. It was one that thrived because neither of them looked too closely at the whys of what had gotten either of them where they were in life. Together they just marked time.

For him, it had grown stale already. He'd begun to think that was because it didn't approach the depth he knew he needed in a relationship that meant forever. He'd guided CJ here in a first step toward doing what he'd been avoiding most of his adult life. He needed to open himself to the pain of the past before he could hope to face any in the future. This place put him in touch with the person he'd been before his fall from grace. A person of family and roots and love.

He'd come a long way from the boy he'd been. Exactly what was missing from the life he'd created for himself was still a mystery to him. He hoped remembering the boy he had been might be the key to becoming the man he needed to be.

"There it is. Lonesome Valley," he told her as they crested the hill near Laurel Glen's western border. The tree line rose to the crest of the rise overlooking the shallow valley below. The fencing that ran though the hollow separated Laurel Glen from its current rental property—the home where his mother was raised.

The house was old and stately. A colonial from the days when brick had been reserved for the wealthy. Though kept in good repair, the barns and stables lay dormant and unused, calling out for the sounds and smells of bygone years.

"Why Lonesome Valley?" CJ asked.

Mischief sidestepped and bumped hindquarters with Queen Morgana. Queeny snorted her displeasure at such a breech of protocol. "Settle down, you misbegotten bag of bones," Cole crooned, and Mischief settled.

"It's a good thing he's unaware of that slur to his ancestry."

Cole chuckled and pointed. "Speaking of ancestry, this is where my mother grew up," he explained, as both horses settled under them. "When I was a kid, the outbuildings felt melancholy to me. Really, the whole place did. It was as if something was missing. So I asked my grandfather why there weren't any horses in the stable and why this place had no name.

"Granddad laughed and said not everyone lived on a farm and few people named their houses. I was about nine and highly insulted that he thought I was so lacking in life experience. I told him I knew a lot of kids whose houses weren't named, but I thought his house should have a name since it was so old and special. So he told me to go ahead and name it if I felt that strongly about it. I thought for a while and, a big fan of westerns and old John Wayne and Roy Rogers movies, I decided on Lonesome Valley."

CJ stepped out of the saddle, and Cole followed suit. "Why that name?" she asked as she tied the Morgan to a tree at the edge of the woods. "I think Charming Valley or Heavenly Valley would be more appropriate."

"Granddad asked the same thing. I told him the barn didn't have a tractor the way it should, the stables didn't have horses, and he and Grandmother were all alone when we weren't there visiting. He got the saddest look on his face. 'Don't live for your children alone, my boy,' he said to me. 'They grow up and they leave you to the empty life you've created for yourself.'"

"So were they really all alone rattling around in that big empty house? Just the two of them?" CJ asked as she sat cross-legged in the cool shade.

Cole sank to the lush grass next to CJ, aware of

her presence so close beside him. "Except for some staff, yeah. They were. I went home that day and asked Granny Taggert why Mom's parents were so lonely. She said that Granddad and Grandmother were older when my mom was born and that they doted on her. They apparently spent all their time and energy on her. They saw friends less and less after she was born because no one their age had children. They pulled back from all their community activities because that would have left her alone. Pretty soon she was their whole world. Then she grew up and got married.

"Even though she just lived next door, they'd lost their center. Mom was busy with her life, and Hope was too little to go off on her own very much, so I went to see them as much as I could. We were pretty close."

"And they died right before your mother?"

Cole nodded, recalling those days when he felt he was the only one who missed them. Life had gone on for the rest of the world without a ripple, and part of his heart seemed to be missing. "Their estate hadn't even been settled yet," he murmured.

"You lost a lot of people who were important to you at that point of your life."

He almost didn't say what needed to be said even though he realized that letting her know the worst of him and the best of him was a prime reason for bringing her there. He forged ahead but grimaced as he admitted, "Fourteen through seventeen weren't good ages for me. I didn't react well to those losses at all. You, on the other hand lost as much, if not more, and handled it so much better than I did.''

CJ did some sort of double-jointed spin onto her knees. Then she was suddenly sitting on her heels facing him. "Why are you so hard on yourself? You were only a child. I was nearly eighteen when my trials started. Those years make a huge maturity difference. Besides which, you were a boy, and boys are years behind females at that point.''

Cole grinned at her attempt to lighten the mood, but he felt the smile slip off his face. Looking past her at the vista below reminded him of those dark days when massive changes had rolled into his life like the thunderheads rolling toward them on the horizon. They seemed to reflect his remembered confusion. His anger. His huge sense of loss. But other things raced across his mind, as well.

"I'm afraid my mother wasn't what—'' He stopped. It felt like a betrayal to even voice his thoughts, but there was no denying the truth about Marley Taggert. She had been spoiled. He could remember that she'd often wanted things Ross would tell her they just couldn't afford yet. Cole had long since figured out that his mother always got those things anyway, if not from *his* father then from *hers*.

"After finding out about Donovan, I wonder if I even knew her,'' he said, nearly choking on the words. "How could someone turn out to be so opposite of what they appeared? Everyone loved her. She had a way of smiling that made you think you were her world. But when Donovan gloated to Dad about his affair with her, he said they'd planned to move to another state. She was leaving us behind.''

''You don't know that he was telling truth or that she would have gone along with it even if that was the plan. Maybe she thought leaving you with your father would be better. Kinder to all three of you. In a way it was the fair thing to do.''

Cole frowned. ''Donovan did say she'd changed her mind about even leaving Dad. He said that was why she rode the horse. She was trying to make up with Dad by settling our argument. I can't imagine why she thought that could repair the damage an affair must have caused between them.''

''There's no way you can know what she was trying to do, what she was thinking, or how your lives would have changed if she had lived. It's futile to try analyzing the ifs in life. Believe me, I've tried. I second-guessed every decision I made about the farm, but in the end I still had to live with losing it. I chose to put it behind me because I realized I needed all my energy to go forward. We all do. If we don't move forward we don't move at all. We stay bogged down in the what ifs and wind up miserable.''

''Like my father did for so long? Like I still am? Like he and I are together? I try. I came back here to try.'' He shook his head. ''But there's an invisible wall between Dad and me that time built. I know most of it is my fault. I blamed him. I cast him in the role of the villain and treated him like my worst enemy. He *was* my worst enemy. I can't get past it.

I love him, but how do I tell him I'm sorry? Especially when all he needs to do is open his mouth, and I'm furious all over again.''

"Well, what are you furious about?"

"A lot of things, apparently, considering the way we argue. I guess…this sounds so stupid. Why was he so busy with everything but Mom? So much so that she went looking elsewhere for what she couldn't get from him?''

"Cole, you can't absolve the dead by casting blame on the living.''

He grimaced. "Is that what I'm doing?'' He didn't give her time to respond. He already knew the answer. "So how do I change this dynamic between us?''

"Maybe you need to tell him to be quiet, since, as much as I've come to like your father, he seems to have a case of terminal foot-in-the-mouth disease where you're concerned. Then just blurt out how you feel. I've thought about doing it myself, but I value my job too much.''

Cole shook his head, uncomfortable with the idea of confronting his father with his deepest thoughts.

"He can't fire you as his son, so what's holding you back? Wouldn't it be better to just seize a moment and tell him it's time the two of you talk? Wouldn't it be better than weeks of tense civility punctuated with moments of irritation and friction?''

He shrugged. "I guess. Like you said. He can't exactly fire me as his son. Amelia wouldn't let him,'' he added, only half joking. "But until after the baby is born, I think any confrontation better wait. Dad's a nervous wreck about her.''

"Time has a way of slipping by, Cole. I've said it before. Just don't wait too long.'' She glanced at the darkening sky. "So tell me, do I get the dime tour of Lonesome Valley before that storm breaks?''

Cole shook his head. "I'm afraid it's occupied until after the fifteenth. Maybe I'll bring you back then.''

"Then why did you bring me here now?''

"Because I want to know you, and I want you to know me. Because I need...'' He hesitated. How much could he say when he wasn't sure what he could give in return? "I need...a friend.''

CJ was stymied. It was the same request he'd made before, but today it felt different. Less superficial, maybe. Less as if she'd been thrown a bone and more like he meant a deeper friendship than he had with anyone else. She didn't know, exactly—just different. Maybe the difference was the edge of desperation in his voice that hadn't been there before. The trouble was she didn't know if she was capable of being just Cole's friend. His was certainly not the request of her dreams, but she had to admit it was better than the hollow feeling she'd been left with since last Thursday.

What about Elizabeth? she wondered suddenly. Wasn't Elizabeth his friend? And more? "What did Elizabeth say when you showed her this place?'' CJ asked.

"Elizabeth?" Cole stared at her, clearly not understanding the point of her question.

"Yes, Elizabeth, the woman you're seeing."

"I haven't brought her here. Why would I?"

"Because…" CJ just stared at him. No, she would be his friend but would not offer advice on his love life. That much of a masochist she wasn't. "No reason. If we're not going down there we'd better get back to the compound. Mischief still isn't too happy with thunderstorms, and I hate riding wet."

CJ took her coffee onto her little front porch the following Saturday morning. It was the first full weekend she'd had off in a month. Unfortunately, the day loomed ahead, empty and boring. Time off left too much time to think. And the one thing she didn't need to do more of was think. She'd done enough of it for ten people since Cole talked her into that ride on Tuesday afternoon. It had taken hours each night to turn her brain off enough to let her sleep, and even then Cole was not only in her thoughts but the star of dreams that left her edgy and needy. And she'd lost count of the times someone had to rouse her from a daydream while she was at work.

She'd tried reading her Bible and praying for peace. She asked for whatever blessing the Lord thought she needed since she had no idea what kind of help to even ask for. But time and again either her thoughts returned to Cole while in prayer or sneaked in and made the sentences in her Bible meaningless. She just couldn't concentrate.

Riding was out because Morning wasn't up to being ridden even though Cole had let her return to the regular stable. The mare's ataxia was almost gone, but she was nowhere near coordinated enough for any real activity. There were Mischief and Demon to work with, but Ross Taggert tended to frown on her working on her days off. And truth be told she'd really wanted to get away from Laurel Glen, where everything reminded her of Cole.

She yawned and propped her crossed ankles on the rail, causing the chair to rock on its rear legs. Maybe she'd be really lazy and take a nap. Maybe, instead of fighting the inevitable, she'd invite Cole into her mind and welcome thoughts of him. Yeah, that just might be the ticket, she decided, already relaxing as she let her eyelids slide closed and her head drop back. She really did need the sleep.

Sometime later the toot of a horn from what sounded like two feet in front of her sent her jumping out of her skin. The back legs of the chair skated forward, her legs flew up in the air and CJ found herself staring at the porch ceiling from an extremely undignified and uncomfortable position.

Footsteps thundered across the wooden porch, echoing in her head. "Are you all right? Are you hurt? I didn't mean to startle you," Cole said in a rush—clearly the offending horn blower. The horrified expression on his face when he bent and started checking her arms and legs for broken bones sent a little bubble of mirth erupting to the surface.

She couldn't help herself. She knew how ridiculous she looked and she certainly knew how foolish Cole looked frantically trying to detect any injury to her inelegant person. Mirth soon gave way to total hilarity even though her body was busy registering and cataloging the feel of his hands checking her arms and legs for broken bones.

"I'm fine," she tried to say but was laughing so hard she doubted he understood.

"Don't move," he said, his husky voice showing that he wasn't unaffected by the physical contact, either.

Luckily there was another level—the silliness of her slide from grace—to fall back on. CJ clung to that aspect of the incident and kept laughing.

"This isn't funny," he groused. She could see he was trying not to acknowledge any attraction to her. Finally he stood, looking annoyed, and smacked his head into a hanging pot of pansies. His laughter erupted as if it had been pent up for centuries. It was a sound that gladdened her heart. If she wanted nothing else for Cole, it was that he be happy.

CJ finally gathered her wits enough to right herself, and Cole got himself under control enough to help her to her feet. Then he bent to pick up the chair and coffee mug. When he straightened their gazes locked. Jocularity fled, leaving their unacknowledged attraction to thicken and charge the air.

The sound of a whimper floating upward through

the floorboards broke the stalemate. Cole froze, his ear cocked toward the wood. "Did you hear that?" he asked. "It came from under the porch. There should be flashlight in the cabinet under the kitchen sink. Could you get it for me?"

CJ nodded, still unable to speak, and ran for the flashlight. She returned to find Cole on his knees next to the steps. He took the light and shone it into the darkness under the porch.

"Well, what have we here?" he asked as he dragged a filthy, growling, fur-covered bag of bones from under the porch.

It was indistinguishable as anything other than an animal. "I haven't a clue," CJ said, meaning it. "It isn't dangerous, is it?"

Holding the snarling fur ball by the scruff of its neck, he turned it this way and that, checking it out. "No. And as a professional guess, I'd say it's a dog. A puppy. Hello, Dangerous," he said, then gave a quiet chuckle and enfolded the little creature against his chest. For several minutes Cole continued to stroke it gently as if fleas didn't leap from their safe haven under his strong hand. "I think what you could use is some TLC," he murmured.

The growling rumble stopped and turned to a quiet, grateful yip. Cole looked at her. There was a mournfulness in his big, onyx eyes so profound that CJ felt her heart nearly melt in her chest. His ability—no, his capacity—to feel the pain of God's creatures great and small, to accept it as his own and then set out to heal it was what she loved most about Cole.

Yes, loved. It was time she faced the truth and admitted that to herself.

"Do you think you could drive me to my office?" he asked quietly. "This fellow needs a bath, food and a good going over medically. Not necessarily in that order. He's in bad shape. I doubt he weighs ten pounds. I'm not even sure he should have been weaned yet."

"Just let me get dressed and grab my license."

Chapter Thirteen

From atop Demon, CJ watched Cole walk toward the stables, Dangerous yipping at his heels. She chuckled as the little dog, in his enthusiasm, tripped his master. The dirty bundle of fur had indeed turned out to be a puppy, in spite of CJ's doubts. Cole was sure the little guy was a purebred, though under-weight, Irish wolfhound.

No record of his origins had turned up even though Cole had called every farm in the area during the last two weeks, trying to find out where the puppy had wandered from. He'd kept the starved wolfhound at his side for the first week, taking him on calls to reassure Dangerous with his constant presence and bottle feeding him a special formula. Dangerous had flourished under Cole's loving attention.

CJ climbed off Demon's back wishing she weren't so jealous of a dog. It wasn't as if Cole's attitude and treatment of her hadn't been more friendly since their ride. He had asked—no, begged—her to be his friend, and she had settled into the role, however reluctantly. She couldn't shake the feeling that in some way she might help him find his way back to the Lord.

But the title friend still chafed and was so much less than she wanted from him. She told herself to be grateful for her blessings, but for once the familiar refrain didn't soothe her troubled spirit. She'd decided not to encourage too much closeness, hoping to guard her heart while keeping herself open to the leading of the Lord.

She turned Demon over to his handler and walked to the edge of the ring to watch Cole. He bent to wrestle with Dangerous and laughed when the pup's long legs got away from him. Dangerous went into an ungainly, tail-over-teacup sprawl in the tall grass, drawing a hearty laugh from Cole as well as from a couple of the men working nearby.

It was plain to see from the love in Cole's eyes that he was now the proud owner of a member of one of the largest dog breeds. Whether he'd planned to adopt a dog or not, Cole had fallen hard for the leggy, underfed puppy. And it was just as clear by the worshipful expression in Dangerous's eyes that nothing would be too great a sacrifice for his hero.

Unfortunately, from what she'd heard Hope and Amelia say, Dangerous caused more problems for his new master than he fixed. And as Cole drew closer, CJ could see the traces of a harried expression on his face. She'd bet dollars to doughnuts Dangerous had them both in hot water again.

"What did he do now?" she asked, bending to scratch behind the puppy's ears. Dangerous immediately dropped and rolled over, presenting his tender belly for attention. CJ hunkered down and complied with a laugh, as unable to resist Dangerous as Cole was.

Cole grimaced. "Is it that obvious that he's done it again?"

"'Fraid so."

He sighed and leaned against the fence, crossing his arms and ankles. "He got out of my bathroom when I went down to grab a quick breakfast. I went upstairs to get him and found the present he'd dragged up the back steps from the kitchen for me. It was the roast Ruth Ann planned for dinner. Phew! Is she ever mad! And Sally's not too happy with the stains on the carpets, either. I told her I'd send someone to clean them, but it didn't do much to appease her. Between the two of them, the little guy barely escaped with his tail intact. Why are my animals always the worst behaved ones around here?" he asked with a sigh.

An unexpected crack of laughter escaped her. She knew his had been a rhetorical question but she couldn't resist answering anyway. "Like father, like sons," CJ told him. "Or they're bad because they know beneath that big strong exterior of yours, *you* are a marshmallow. Mischief and Dangerous both have you figured out. And, for the record, so do I."

"Ha, ha. Very funny." Cole grumbled then smiled, letting her know he recognized her teasing as all in fun. Then he surprised her completely by saying, "I had Ruth Ann pack a picnic lunch. Thought getting my pal here safely out of the house and away from the compound would be a good idea. There's enough for two. You feel like coming along?"

"You aren't riding with Elizabeth today?"

"She's tied up. Besides, I asked *you*."

CJ knew she should say no. She'd thought long and hard about the strain having Cole for a friend would be, but she still found herself nodding. "I don't have anything else planned, so sure," she told him, not wanting him to think she was changing any plans to accommodate his last-minute invitation. Her mother had always told her not to accept last-minute dates. But, she reminded herself, this was not a date.

Cole congratulated himself as he finished saddling Mischief. After tucking Dangerous in a sling across his chest, he went to meet CJ where she waited with Queen Morgana. She sat straight in the saddle and ready to ride, her golden hair gleaming in the summer sunlight. He pointed them toward the stream near the southern border of the property, and they started what was a good half-hour ride at a leisurely pace.

"I didn't know Laurel Glen's border extended this far," CJ commented as they approached what had once been the site of many a Taggert family picnic.

Those were days he still had trouble remembering without the pain of their loss tainting them. What was worse was that he was furious at having those precious hours stolen and frustrated because he didn't know who to be angry with anymore.

He had once been consumed with anger at Ross, and now he knew he'd been wrong. The anger should have transferred itself to his mother, and some of it had, but not all and certainly not in the same way. He knew that was wrong. His mother had been the one at fault yet he couldn't summon as much anger toward her as he had toward Ross.

True, he'd believed his father capable of murder for nearly a year. Then, when Cole had proved to himself the error of his thinking, he'd thought Ross so uncaring that he'd driven Marley to suicide. Now he knew his father had been the injured party, and still his anger continued. He wished he understood why.

"Oh, this is beautiful," CJ said as they entered the glen that had helped give the farm its name.

"It was this spot that named the farm. My great-grandmother transplanted all that mountain laurel lining the entrance drive from right around here. I guess you could say this was the original Laurel Glen."

"Then it wasn't always called Laurel Glen?" CJ asked.

"Not until Granny Taggert." He chuckled remembering the feisty older woman. "She decided the place needed a name with a little more zip than the

Taggert farm. My great-grandmother took no prisoners.''

"I wondered about the mountain laurel. It's a little impractical,'' CJ said.

Cole laughed. "It's more than impractical, and you know it. It's downright dangerous, but no one, least of all me, who should know better, wants to change it. Granny's memory is worth double fencing and extra patrols.''

"I wish I could have known her. She sounds as if she was a great old gal.''

"I wish you could have, too. That would mean she'd still be with us, and I'd have the chance to make up to her for disappointing her at the end of her life. That may be my greatest regret. Death is so final, and I was only thinking of myself in those days.''

"If she was as wise as everyone says I'll bet she knew you'd eventually pull it all together. And you have.'' CJ stood in the stirrups and looked around. "Is that the stream where you and Jeff took your mud baths?''

"Yeah,'' he admitted, trying to keep the embarrassment from his voice. "I haven't been here in some time.''

"I don't know how you've stayed away.''

Cole slid to the ground and tied Mischief to a low-hanging branch, his feeling of melancholy returning. He walked ahead silently. He'd come here with Hope a couple of days after his return to Laurel Glen the winter before last and had experienced the same thing. It felt more like a haunted place than the sacred one of his childhood. He narrowed his eyes and with a hand on his hip looked around, trying to figure out what had changed since that day. It was still a beautiful and calming scene right off a greeting card, but something was different.

Then he realized what it was. Another tree near the ones his father had planted in honor of his parents and Granny Taggert had been added. It was a big tree, not a sapling, and looked as if it had been there as long as Granny's. He walked over and read the plaque aloud. "'In honor of Marley Taggert. Wife and loving mother.' I guess he finally managed to put her behind him," he muttered. Even now, as much as he wanted his father and Amelia to be happy, he didn't know how he felt about his vibrant mother having been relegated to a mere memory.

"I thought you wanted that for your father. Why so angry?"

He hadn't even realized he *was* angry, but he was, and there was no use denying it. "He had no right to keep it a secret," Cole blurted. "He should have told us the truth. Why would he let me hate him? Why would he let me go on blaming him all those years? I needed him. I needed this place and its memories. I needed a home and roots."

"Maybe that's why he kept silent. Maybe he was trying not to taint your memories of your mother with what she did to him."

"I had a right to know. I feel as if my whole life has been a lie or at least based on one."

"If I understand the situation correctly your father was in a no-win situation. If he'd told you that your mother had decided to leave him and both their children for another man, he would have been speaking ill of a dead woman who couldn't defend herself. A woman whose death he felt responsible for. A woman he apparently loved very much. Your father is a very protective man. I can't imagine him hurting his children with knowledge like that."

"I know," Cole said on a sigh. "I know that in my head." He thumped his chest over his heart with closed fist. "But here there's this anger still burning. How do I get rid of it? I know now it's misplaced."

CJ considered him, her golden eyes full of compassion and hesitation. Finally, she nodded as if listening to some inner voice. "Okay. Remember, you asked." She took a deep breath and gazed at him intently as if willing him to understand what she was about to say. "You go to the Lord and you tell Him you're sorry about your anger toward Him and toward your father. You ask Him to take the anger and destroy it. Then you go to your father and talk about what happened. This gulf between you wasn't created by any one person. It took at least three of you to dig it, but one of you has to make the first move to cross it."

Cole knew she was right about talking to his father. He knew she was right about who was at fault. But he wasn't sure about the God thing. He still felt abandoned and disappointed to have been ignored and, yes, terribly—horribly—angry that his mother was dead.

"I can't talk to my father yet. I can't explain it, but I don't think he can take a confrontation right now. Something's, if not wrong, then at least not right, but I can't put my finger on what it could be. I've asked pointed questions, and he's denied any problems. He says business is fine. He says his finances are fine. He says Amelia's fine and that he isn't worried about the baby. I guess he could still be a little concerned about being a father again because of his age, but this feels like more.

"All I know is right now we have a kind of fragile cease-fire between us. It's nothing we agreed upon. It just sort of blossomed since the night Morning got sick. I don't react to anything he says in anger anymore even if I feel it, and he does the same."

"That's certainly a step in the right direction."

"But still, until the baby's born, I'm afraid to rock the boat with even five minutes of touchy conversation."

"Don't wait too long, Cole," CJ cautioned once again.

But this time Cole felt an ominous roiling in his stomach at her familiar warning. He shook his head. "I won't. As soon as I see him get a little more relaxed, I'll talk to him."

"And God?"

"Him I'm not ready to deal with, either."

Cole stopped the SUV near CJ's battered old truck. He didn't know if he was ready for this, but it had been several days since the picnic and he was more drawn to CJ than ever. He'd managed to appear at the stable the following evening just as CJ prepared to ride Morning for the first time.

He'd invited himself along as a medical escort— just in case something was still wrong with the palomino. Nothing had been, of course. He'd never have let the animal out of her stall if he had the slightest doubt that she was ready to be ridden. It had been an excuse to share a little time with CJ.

Aunt Meg had cooperated by inviting her to dinner on Monday, just as Dangerous had helped on Tuesday when he'd charged out of the car, through a mud puddle and into CJ's arms.

Cole smiled, remembering the way she'd dismissed his need to apologize and laughed as Dangerous's muddy paws streaked across her cheeks. Laughing all the way into her bathroom at the puppy's shenanigans, she'd taken Dangerous into the shower with her.

While waiting on her porch, Cole had realized he was ridiculously jealous of a dog. He'd made up his mind then and there to take the relationship he was trying to build with CJ one step further. He'd sought Elizabeth's opinion on how best to accomplish that, and she suggested he ask CJ out on a casual last-minute date. She'd said no woman would be encouraged to think there was any promise of a future in a last-minute date.

So here it was, Friday night, and he was poised to

ask her out and feeling uncomfortably like a high school kid. Cole looked down and realized Dangerous was licking his master's sweaty palms. This was ridiculous. He hadn't been this nervous when he'd asked Jeannie Sheldon, the most popular girl in school, to the sophomore dance! Shaking his head, Cole climbed out of the SUV and went in search of CJ.

It was Dangerous who found her sitting on her back step. Her hair was wet, and she was wearing pale blue shorts and a T-shirt. She looked cool in spite of the oppressive end-of-July heat and humidity. He watched her rubbing the puppy's tender belly and chuckling at his tail-wagging antics.

"You mean all I have to do is fall down on my back and you'll finally notice me?" Cole joked.

CJ didn't look up but continued petting Dangerous. "He needs all the loving attention he can get. You, on the other hand, have enough ego for three men."

"You wound me," Cole accused. "Have you no idea how insecure I am?" He crouched next to her and the ecstatic puppy. He didn't know how he wound up holding her hand. She'd been petting Dangerous, then she was staring into his eyes, her golden gaze locked with his. He drew little circles with his thumb on the tender skin of the inside of her wrist.

"Cole?" she asked, clearly confused.

No more confused than he. "I, um, I have tickets to *Crazy For You* in Wilmington tonight," he said, going automatically into the speech Elizabeth had helped him prepare. "Would you like to see it?"

"Wouldn't you rather take Elizabeth? Or is she busy?" CJ asked and swallowed visibly. She was obviously befuddled by his invitation, and he didn't know if that was a good thing or not. She shouldn't be so willing to take a back seat to any other woman. "I didn't ask Elizabeth," he told her. "I asked you. Do you want to go?"

CJ nodded.

He gave a sharp nod of his own and stood, scooping Dangerous into his arms. "Great," he said. "I'll just leave this monster in his crate in the clinic. That ought to keep him out of trouble while we're gone. I can pick him up on the way back home. I'll be by for you around six-thirty. Is that time enough?"

Again, she only nodded, her eyes wide.

Cole beat a hasty retreat and half an hour later shrugged into his sports jacket and straightened his tie. He fisted his hands, trying to stop them from shaking. He was still as nervous as a cat in a room full of rocking chairs. He told himself there was no reason to be so anxious. Asking CJ out on a date might not have been the best strategic move but it still felt right.

She was special and deserved to be treated as such. As far as he could see no one saw her the way he did. To his father she was a good worker and a talented trainer. To Amelia and Hope she was a new friend. But to him CJ was happiness, warmth and passion. Just looking into her eyes gladdened his heart and warmed his soul. For the first time in his life Cole wanted to take a chance on a future that included another person. He wanted a love that would never end. He wanted to be able to give his love without reservation.

His phone rang, drawing his attention. Hoping it wasn't an emergency, he lifted the receiver. "Hi, Cole," Elizabeth said. "How did it go?"

"I did it."

"I take it I'm no longer your safety net."

He felt butterflies return to his stomach. "I wouldn't go that far. I don't want her to get hurt if it turns out that I don't feel all for her I should. I thought I'd just sort of avoid the subject of you until I was more sure of where I'm headed."

"I just thought I should warn you. I've sort of been rethinking our conversation. I'm not sure someone like CJ can spend time with a man she's attracted to and not at least hope for a future. Go slow. You know?"

Cole felt his hackles rise. What did she take him for? "I'm not about to rush her into bed. I'm not that out of touch with who she is."

"A kiss for someone like CJ could be as intimate as a whole lot more for the rest of us." Elizabeth sounded so sad. Not for the first time Cole condemned those who'd hurt her, who'd made her think she deserved less, was worth less, than others.

"Since when do we put you in a category different from the one Hope and CJ belong in? Just because you have an unearned reputation doesn't make it a real one.''

''We aren't talking about me. We're trying to safeguard CJ's heart until you're able to risk your own. So have a good time. Have lots of laughs. Just don't get too serious too fast.''

Chapter Fourteen

CJ hadn't French braided her hair in years. And as she finished with it, she decided she liked it. It was a practical hairstyle she'd often worn in competition. It stayed together well while looking a little fancier than her usual braid or ponytail. It was too much trouble for everyday, of course, but then tonight wasn't everyday for her.

Tonight was a milestone. She was going to a play with the man she loved.

She cautioned herself not to put any meaning on this night from Cole's standpoint. Surely Elizabeth must've been busy or he never would have asked her to go along. CJ knew how much he hated to be at loose ends. That's probably why he'd asked her to go, but whatever the reason, she intended to savor the night and tuck the memories away for another day.

As she slid into her shoes, Cole knocked on her

front door. She frowned at her reflection, rather surprised he'd knock instead of just tooting his horn out
front. An invitation to a play, knocking at the door—
she would almost say this was a real date instead of
two friends with nothing better to do than spending
the evening with each other.

CJ forced her mind off possibilities. She shrugged
and walked toward her front door. More than likely
his mother and the infamous Granny Taggert had
taught him from an early age that beeping for anyone, even just a friend, wasn't proper.

She opened the door and her heart skipped. Cole
stood on her little porch, as tall and handsome as he
always was. She just hadn't counted on the impact
of seeing him in a sports coat and tie. He wore a
shirt, tie and light blue linen jacket over black slacks
with knife-edge creases. The tan he got from so much
outdoor work looked darker and more sophisticated
in the GQ outfit.

"Ready?" he asked and smiled, his dark eyes saying something CJ simply couldn't identify. She swallowed. Why did this suddenly feel like a real date?

Minutes into the ride to Wilmington's exclusive
Hotel DuPont, CJ's nervousness fled as they talked
about the kinds of things they always did these days
when they ran into each other at Laurel Glen. He
told her about his day and Dangerous's latest antics,
then she recounted hers. It was just like always. They
were only friends.

CJ made a concerted effort not to look too wide-
eyed as they entered the elegant lobby, and she

thought she'd done a good job. Then Cole settled his hand at the small of her back. His touch set her nerve endings jangling, and her stomach felt as if she had just fallen thirty stories.

"What?" She gasped and whirled to face him.

Cole grinned and looked entirely too pleased by her overreaction. But he didn't comment on the obvious. Instead he waved a hand ahead of them toward the restaurant. "Did you think I was going to starve you?"

"I—I'd forgotten about dinner," she said and could have kicked herself for admitting his invitation had thrown her for a loop enough that she'd forgotten about eating. Then she saw the restaurant and just managed to keep herself from gasping. How was she going to afford this? Her truck needed so much work the mechanic suggested the best way to fix the problem would be to call a car dealership and a junkyard. Not necessarily in that order.

"I'm relieved," Cole said. "I wouldn't want you to miss the food here. It's even better than the atmosphere."

A maître d' stepped up to a podium in the doorway, and CJ stifled a giggle. The man looked more like a palace guard than a glorified waiter.

Cole fought a smile of his own. "Reservation for Taggert," he told the man. With a flourish and what CJ was sure was a phony French accent, he showed them to a table and presented them with menus. When she looked at hers she felt ill.

"Uh, Cole, my menu hasn't got any prices," she

whispered, not wanting anyone else to hear. "I thought this custom went out with the Dark Ages. How am I supposed to know what to order? Suppose I order something and I don't have enough money to pay for it?"

Cole blinked and narrowed his dark eyes a bit, then a look of profound sadness settled on his features. He shook his head and set his menu to the side. He took hers and stacked it with his before taking her hand. "I've come to know you pretty well these last weeks," he said, his eyes soft. "That's why I asked the maître d' to give you a special menu without prices. I wanted you to relax. I didn't want you to worry about what tonight is costing, and I knew you would."

"But—" she started to protest.

Cole put his finger against her lips to silence her protest. "When I take a woman out, I pay. Call it a Taggert family tradition."

"Oh," CJ said, her face heating and her mind in a whirl. He made it sound as if this really *was* a date. She wished she had the nerve to ask him.

"Any more dumb questions?" he asked, once again having taken her hand.

CJ shrugged. "What's the play about?" she asked, too cowardly to ask for the answer she really wanted.

Cole chuckled. "It's a musical comedy that was written around several Gershwin tunes. It's set in a desert mining town or something like that. The hero is a big-city boy trying to prove himself. He's out on his own far from his interfering mother, and the heroine is the local girl he falls for. I think you'll like it.''

And she did. After those first few awkward moments at the restaurant they fell into the kind of conversation they always enjoyed. The play was funny, the seats excellent, and they both laughed at the antics onstage. On the way home they got into silly speculations about the period in history when cities had become quite modern but the country was still primitive. They decided back then traveling must have seemed like moving from one kind of world to another.

It wasn't until Cole turned into the drive at Laurel Glen that her nerves reappeared. Would he take this date scenario as far as a good-night kiss? She still dreamed about that kiss in the clinic and woke each time feeling the loss of his nearness. Though she longed for more between them than the friendship Cole had ultimately asked for, she told herself often that he'd been wise to limit them to friendship alone.

CJ knew there would have been more consequences for her than for him if they'd moved beyond it and the relationship hadn't worked out. Laurel Glen was, after all, Cole's home, and if someone had to leave it would be her.

Unfortunately, the closer they got to Laurel Glen the edgier she got. She wasn't sure if what she was feeling was anticipation because she wanted him to kiss her no matter what or anxiety because she feared the consequences.

Whatever the cause of her uneasiness, Cole had

barely brought the SUV to a stop when CJ reached for the door handle. Only Cole's hand on her shoulder stopped her from bolting from the vehicle for her front door.

"In these parts, ma'am," Cole said in a bad Western accent, "young ladies let their escorts open car doors for them, and their escorts are duty bound to walk them to their front porch. It goes along with paying for the dinner."

Thinking quickly to cover her nervousness, she aped his accent. "Well, now, they surely do want you menfolk to work in these parts, don't they?"

Cole laughed and slid from the car, appearing by her side in moments. As they walked to her door, he once again put his hand at her waist. This time, though her heartbeat accelerated, CJ didn't gasp or move away.

At the door, she fumbled with the lock and Cole covered her hand with his. "Here. Let me get that for you," he said, his voice just above a whisper.

As he handled the often difficult lock, she realized the warmth of his nearness was affecting her as much as his touch had. She looked into his face, and her breath caught as his gaze met hers. The porch light made his eyes look darker and more compelling than usual. And there was something in his expression that had her heart beating out of control.

"There's another custom I don't think I'm going to be able to let slip by, either," Cole whispered, his voice more husky than she'd ever heard it before.

"C-custom?" she asked, her voice sounding like

an unfortunate squeak. Cole didn't seem to mind. He smiled, his teeth gleaming in the porch light. Then the grin faded and he bent his head, clearly intending to press his lips to hers. CJ held her breath, wondering if this kiss would cause the same riot of sensations inside her that the last one had.

She wasn't at all surprised when it did. Then he moved closer, his arms wrapping around her and gathering her into his embrace. CJ found herself unready for the wildfire that burned out of control within her body.

Not ready at all.

Cole heard a little sound escape CJ's throat as his arms tightened around her waist. The fog that had descended on his brain cleared just a little. He didn't know if that moan was an objection or encouragement, but he knew he'd treaded on dangerous ground. Moved too fast for her and for him. He broke the kiss and stepped back, his stomach turning to stone.

"I didn't mean—" The apology died on his lips when he saw the dreamy look in CJ's eyes.

Elizabeth was right. There was no halfway with a woman like CJ. He either had to court her with the promise of marriage or he had to stay away. For both their sakes, till he was sure of himself, he'd better choose staying away. He wasn't ready for white lace and promises.

Unsure what to say, he shook his head, turned and walked away.

* * *

"Okay, let me get this straight," Cole said to Elizabeth the next afternoon. "You want me to ask CJ to attend the charity dance the night before Graystone's cross-country." He shook his head in disbelief. "Elizabeth, I just got through telling you I've decided not to pursue CJ further till I'm more sure of me."

"And I told you you're an idiot!" She shot the words back.

Cole ignored the comment just as he had the last time she commented on his decision regarding CJ. Instead he went on as if Elizabeth hadn't spoken. "As for that race or whatever Graystone and your father want to call it, you know how I feel about that event, benefit or not. Last year I took care of three good animals hurt because of it. They were all in a lot of pain. One I had to put down. And all because that nitwit Graystone doesn't care who gets hurt as long as he keeps his standing as designer of the toughest course of the year."

"Charles Graystone isn't the one who hurt those animals. It was the fault of their riders or the owners who entered them when they weren't ready. Daddy rides that course with Charles as it's being laid out. It isn't impossible."

"Not any one component of it, no. But as a whole, by the time the horses get to the end, the jumps and hazards are too tough. Taking their animals bungee jumping off the Delaware Memorial Bridge would be safer."

Elizabeth smirked. "Well, not everyone at Laurel Glen seems to agree with you. Your father entered this year with Ross's Prize."

Cole felt the blood drain from his head. His whole body went hot then cold. "That isn't funny, Lizzie," Cole snapped, tired of her mercurial attitude.

Elizabeth bristled at the nickname given to her as a teen by their peers. Cole felt a little guilty taking his annoyance out on her. Before he could apologize, her green eyes flashed, and she smacked the fashion magazines she'd been looking through onto the coffee table. Cole grabbed her hand as she stood to walk away. "I'm sorry."

"That was uncalled for, Cole."

"I know, and I'm really sorry. I guess I forgot you're not supposed to shoot the messenger. Look, I've got to go talk my father out of this."

"When was the last time you talked your father out of anything? Why waste your time? Better to spend your time remembering that Jeff and Hope will be going to that charity dance because Graystone's daughter is one of their students. And obviously Amelia and Ross will be going since he's a participant. That's going to leave CJ sitting at home, as usual, while all her friends are off dancing the night away. Either that or Jack Alton will take her. I understand Ross bought enough tickets for his professionals and his whole family."

Cole gritted his teeth, refusing to let her see how hard her mention of Alton anywhere near CJ hit him. He stood. "If you'll excuse me, I'm going home to tell my father that this is one family member who isn't going to fall in line with his plans and condone Graystone's suicide race.''

She waved her perfectly manicured hand, dismissing him as she dropped down and picked up her magazines. ''Fine,'' she said. ''Just remember it's your fault if CJ goes with Jack.''

Elizabeth's warning replayed itself in his head during the whole drive home. He parked in the lot near the stable compound, assuming his father would be in his office or somewhere nearby working with the horses. He stalked toward the barn building but stopped short when he heard none other than Jack Alton calling to him.

Cole still hadn't heard anything from Jim Lovell about Laurel Glen's new foreman. Jim had been unable to get any more information on the man than his application and references revealed, so he'd decided to take the investigation a step further. With an excess of vacation time on his hands, Lovell decided to fly to Colorado and rent a car so he could do some in-person snooping. When Cole had protested that it was too much, Lovell had laughed and called it a busman's holiday. Cole knew the detective wanted desperately to make up for mistakenly suspecting him last summer instead of uncovering Harry Donovan's perfidy in the series of crimes that had so badly damaged Laurel Glen's reputation. He was sorry now that he'd troubled the man.

''Is there a problem?'' Cole asked Alton when the foreman caught up to him.

"Problem? No. I just don't want to step on your toes. Your father told me I'm expected to attend some sort of affair next Saturday night. He hinted that he'd like me to bring a guest and, well, if you're not going to be asking CJ, then I thought I would."

Cole didn't like the feeling of anger and jealousy that ripped through him, but this time he recognized it for what it was. Suddenly he wasn't so sure of his decision not to attend the dance. Or the one where he stuck strictly to friendship with CJ. One thing was for sure, there was no way he was going to pass her into this or any man's arms without a fight. "Actually I do intend to ask her," he found himself saying.

Oddly, Alton smiled at his reply. "Good. Then I guess I'll give Elizabeth Boyer a call. Man, oh, man, you surely do seem to have a monopoly on all the pretty women around these parts. I just wondered which one you asked out for that night. Thanks for the heads up," he said with a mysterious smirk. He saluted Cole with his Stetson and walked away.

Cole stood with his fingertips digging into his hips watching Jack Alton stroll away. Boy, that guy really got his goat! Before he was observed standing there vibrating with anger, Cole pivoted and stomped toward the barn.

He found his father in CJ's office deep in discussion.

"Excuse me, CJ. Dad, I need to talk to you. It's about the Graystone cross-country."

"Come on in," Ross ordered. "That's what we were just discussing. CJ's been working with both me and Prize. We're going to keep at it right up until the event.''

Cole took a deep breath. ''I think we should talk in your office,'' he suggested, not wanting to get into another disagreement with his father in front of CJ.

''I doubt there's anything you can't say in front of CJ. This is business, after all.''

''Will it be business when Amelia is stuck raising your orphaned kid alone, and I'm putting Prize down because you got him hurt in this stupid event?''

Ross frowned. ''I have to do something to give this place another shot in the arm. Winning—even finishing—Graystone's cross-country is a boost Laurel Glen could use right now.''

''This is crazy, Dad. Laurel Glen has always ignored Graystone and his lunatic event. You know what happened last year. The man has no regard for safety and no conscience whatsoever about the danger he places the riders and horses in. I can't believe Amelia isn't having fits over this. How can you worry her this way?''

Ross stood, his hands bunched in fists. ''Amelia has no idea this race is anything more than a normal charity cross-country, and I want to keep it that way. I expect you to keep your mouth shut about your objections. I also expect you to attend the ball the night before at Graystone Manor and the event itself. You say you want to be a part of this family. Act like it. We have to present a united front. Laurel Glen needs this.''

"*This* is nuts!" Cole shouted at his father's back as Ross pushed past him and left the office.

Cole swung to face CJ when he heard her disgusted sigh.

"You two aren't like oil and water," she muttered. "You're more like bleach and ammonia. Deadly! Poisonous! I thought you didn't want to upset him right now."

"If you knew what that course was like, you'd understand. He's going to get himself or that horse killed, and that isn't going to do Laurel Glen a bit of good."

"Cole, I've ridden some of the toughest courses in the country and worked with horsemen on all of them. Believe me, Prize is up to this. And your father is an incredible horseman. They'll both be fine."

"You don't get it! This guy designs this course to break the horses and riders. Yeah, some of them make it through okay. And some of them have the brains to drop out. But others push on past the physical limits of both horse and rider. Two men wound up at the hospital last year."

"So what you're saying to me that you didn't say to your father is that you're worried about him."

Cole threw his hands up. "Well, of course I'm worried."

"Too bad you didn't just say that." CJ paused. "Look. I'm sorry this has you worried. But I doubt anything could change his mind about this. I promise I'll do my best to make sure they're up to the task. And in the meantime, maybe you could make sure

Ross understands that you're only worried about him.''

Cole took a deep breath. How did he always get so off track talking to his father? He sighed. "I'll try.''

"Can I do anything else for you?'' she asked, clearly dismissing him.

"You could ride over to Graystone Manor the night of the charity dance with me and keep me from saying anything outrageous to Charles Graystone on the way through the receiving line.''

"Should I bring along a gag and handcuffs?'' she asked with a wry smile.

"A sharp stick should do just fine.'' Cole grimaced, sighed then raised his right hand. "I swear to be on my best behavior, ma'am.''

"I just saw your best behavior, remember. What about Elizabeth?''

He pretended confusion once more. "Elizabeth?''

"Is she unavailable again?''

"She's going with Jack Alton,'' he replied with a careless shrug. If it wouldn't leave such a bad taste in his mouth, he'd thank Alton for the help in keeping the myth that she was a stand-in for Elizabeth alive in CJ's mind. He didn't like her assuming she took a back seat to anyone, but it kept CJ safer from heartbreak if she still thought of him and Elizabeth as a couple, however loosely linked. He wished he could trust himself as much as he trusted CJ, because right then he desperately needed to just hold her and reassure her and have her reassure him.

"Okay," she agreed. "I could use the ride. The pickup's still on the injured list. Besides which, I don't think Old Red is exactly the image your father's striving to foster for Laurel Glen."

Chapter Fifteen

~⟆~

The morning of the Graystone Charity Ball, CJ lay on her sofa staring at the ceiling. It was a week after she'd watched Cole confront Ross in her office, and she was still reeling from the abrupt changes Cole had made in his life—and, consequently, hers.

He'd surprised everyone by moving out of Laurel House and into the recently vacated house his grandparents had once owned. It was the one he'd shown her on the property he called Lonesome Valley. She couldn't help feeling it was ironic that the pretty brick home once again had a lone resident.

When CJ asked him why he'd decided to move, he'd said he just couldn't be around Amelia and not tell her the Graystone event was dangerous. Additionally, he'd said he worried the tension between him and Ross was too much strain for her so near the end of her pregnancy. He'd added that it was taking too much of a toll on him, too, which confused

CJ. Why did he feel overwhelmed by the stress he'd once admitted he was able to ignore?

She had tried again to allay his fears about the upcoming cross-country, but it had been a waste of time. Cole was nothing if not stubborn—a trait he'd inherited from his father. CJ respected Cole's stand on the event even though she didn't agree with him about the severity of the danger.

He was a leisure rider, and a very good one. But it wasn't his profession. Cole's profession was caring for sick and injured animals, and she'd found that veterinarians often frowned on anything that taxed their patients as much as competitive sports do. Doctors were no different where human athletes were concerned. Also, while she was sure Cole would never admit it, she thought he overreacted to the dangers of event riding because of his mother's death and the riding accident that had left Jeff Carrington paralyzed for months.

CJ had seen Cole often during the last week, and seeing him was as confusing as New Year's Eve at Times Square! He kept her so off balance she didn't know which way was up. He'd made no mention of the kiss or anything else about their non date, including his abortive apology for the kiss and his sudden withdrawal from her porch. Nor had he mentioned the charity ball tonight except to tell her what time he'd be by for her. By last night she'd decided her status as Elizabeth's stand-in was well established.

Then this morning he'd sent her flowers!

She ordered herself, for the tenth time since they'd arrived, to remember she was not his type. Elizabeth was Cole's type. She was high heels and evening gowns. CJ was dung-covered boots and jeans. She told herself he probably sent flowers to anyone he was escorting to a charity ball, and he'd be appalled if she attached any importance to them. He'd also be appalled if he knew she had those lovely, expensive flowers in an old mayonnaise jar on her dresser.

Getting to her feet, CJ walked to her closet once again and tried to decide what to wear to the stupid ball. Too bad there'd never really been a Cinderella or a fairy godmother. She could use a little help about now.

Normally she'd wear her black velvet jeans and a silk blouse to a fancy affair with confidence. But wasn't there some stupid rule about velvet in summer? "What does it matter, anyway?" she grumbled. "The place is sure to be air-conditioned."

I bet Elizabeth Boyer doesn't have this problem. She can probably just walk to her closet, close her eyes and wear what her hand falls on.

A knock on her door drew CJ's attention. She assumed it was Hope. No one else came knocking on her door. She never expected to find who she did— the very person whose closet she'd just coveted. She couldn't have been more surprised if she'd opened her door to her mythical Cinderella.

"E-Elizabeth. Hello."

"Hello to you," Elizabeth said with a sunny smile. "I just stopped by for some girl talk."

"Girl talk?" What on earth was girl talk, anyway? CJ wondered. A friend in high school had once called her, practically in tears, to say she was having a bad hair day. Did this have anything to do with that mysterious affliction? CJ sincerely hoped not. That was a concept that still escaped her all these years later. Hair was hair. You got up, you washed it, you braided it and forgot it. How could something that simple suddenly go bad—and for only a day?

"You're hopeless," Elizabeth said, clearly realizing CJ was at sea with the concept. "We talk about what we're wearing tonight. About how good a kisser Cole is. About how cute Jack is. Maybe we do our nails. Talk about the latest fashion don'ts. *Girl talk.*"

"Oh. *Girl talk,*" CJ parroted and felt her stomach roll. And she'd thought what to wear tonight was a problem. She backed into her little parlor and gestured toward the sofa, inviting Elizabeth to sit. "I thought you hated Jack?" she asked.

Elizabeth rolled her eyes. "If I hated him, why would I accept a date with him for tonight?"

CJ wrinkled her nose. "I'm not very good at this. Or fashion," she said hesitantly and with an apologetic shrug. "And I've never done my nails. But Cole kisses very nicely. More than nicely, actually," she added, not wanting to insult the man she loved. "Of course I don't have anyone to compare him with except my ex-boss's son, and he wasn't exactly someone I wanted to kiss me in the first place. But then if Cole's thinking about you and kissing me I don't want him kissing me, either. It would—''

"Stop!" Elizabeth shouted then stared at her for so long CJ began to feel like a bug under a microscope. "You were babbling, pet." She patted the seat next to her. "Come sit down. We need to get a few things straight. First, Cole doesn't think about me when he's with you. I can't, however, claim the opposite since you're all he talks about these days. I'm an excuse, and that's all.

"So here's the deal. I'm here to make sure tonight pushes Cole over the edge. What do you plan to wear?''

CJ frowned. Did she want Cole pushed over an edge where she was concerned? "What edge? What does he say about me and how are you an excuse?" she asked, more confused than ever.

Elizabeth grimaced. "Cole is my friend so I can't really say. That would be breaking a confidence and too close to betrayal."

"But pushing him over some sort of edge isn't betrayal?''

"Not at all. It's engineering a certain atmosphere that will benefit him. Because whether he's ready to admit it or not, you would be good for him. I'm just trying to do something for a friend. So tell me, what are you wearing?''

"Well, I've only really got one thing—a pair of velvet jeans and a silk blouse."

Elizabeth laughed. "Okay, now quit kidding me. This isn't going to work if you don't cooperate."

"Who's kidding?" CJ asked, a really sick feeling invading her stomach. Her clothes were laughable? Maybe she would just plead a headache, stay home, baby-sit Dangerous and solve the whole problem.

Elizabeth stood and charged down the hall toward the bedroom, and CJ jumped up to follow. "Look, let's forget this," she protested.

By the time CJ got to her bedroom, Elizabeth was pivoting to face her, a look of horror written on the beautiful debutante's features. "For Pete's sake. I've never seen so many pairs of jeans in one closet. It looks like a denim explosion in there."

"I think I'll just stay home."

Elizabeth crossed her arms and rubbed her chin with her thumb and crooked index finger while walking around CJ several times, studying her. CJ again felt like a bug being examined. "Don't worry. I can work miracles with a makeup brush and a blow dryer."

CJ groaned. "This sounds like torture."

"Would a little torture be worth getting Cole to admit he has feelings for you?"

"Well, yes, if he had any it would, but—"

"No buts!" Elizabeth looked at the contents of the closet and pawed though them for a few long moments. "Uh-oh. I at least need something to work with, and this is hopeless," she complained. "You're not anywhere near my size." Then her eyes widened. "Not hopeless. Hope!" Elizabeth shouted. "We have to call Hope. Where's your phone?"

It was noon when the Lavender Hill Equestrian

School's minivan pulled up to the cottage. CJ watched Elizabeth go out to greet Hope. They talked for several minutes before both women came in with their arms full of clothes, which they dumped on the parlor chairs.

"And now it begins," Hope said with a mischievous grin.

"I don't know about this, you two," CJ said, backing away from them as they walked toward her.

"We do," they said in unison and kept on coming.

Four hours later CJ stared at the stranger in the mirror. She'd been stuffed into a bathtub full of gardenia-scented bubbles and oil. Her hair had been shampooed and conditioned, then trimmed and styled. They'd given her a manicure and a pedicure and smeared her with lotion from head to foot. And she'd lost count of the number of dresses and pairs of shoes she'd tried on.

Her hair was piled on top of her head with loose curls falling from the center of a thick twisted rope of hair that was looped around the crown of her head. Elizabeth had cut tendrils to frame her face with loose curls. And she was also responsible for the makeup that made CJ feel as if she were ready to go on stage.

Hope had, of course, supplied the dress the two women had decided most flattered her figure. It amazed CJ that Elizabeth had been able to tell she and Hope would be the same size were Hope not a month shy of delivery.

It had been a fun day in its way. CJ hadn't shared

such cherished moments of camaraderie with other women since her mother was killed. The two women had put aside their differences to buff, polish and perfume her within an inch of her life while laughing and becoming friends before CJ's eyes.

Now these two lovely new friends of hers were waiting with palpable anticipation for her verdict on their hard work. And all because they'd tricked her into admitting she was in love with Cole.

"So? Say something," Elizabeth demanded.

"Uh. I guess you could say I'm speechless. It's great. Really. But how is looking like someone else going to make Cole admit he cares for me?"

"You look beautiful. And you don't look like someone else," Hope said. "You look as if you've tried to look your very best and succeeded."

"But this was so much trouble. And if he notices *this* person, and cares for *this* person, then he's noticing someone else and caring for someone else."

Hope stepped behind her so both of them were reflected in the full-length mirror that hung on the back of the bathroom door. "It took this same kind of makeover to get Jeff to stop seeing me as a little girl."

"And ask Hope what I looked like before my mother decided to find out if there was a way to improve on Mother Nature's unexplainable mistake," Elizabeth confided, her voice a little sad and wistful.

Hope frowned and stared at Elizabeth. "You know, everyone is always talking about you before your metamorphosis, but I don't remember you as anything but a butterfly."

"The caterpillar inside me thanks you, my dear."

"CJ, think of it as Cole's wake-up call," Hope said. "Because when all the men are lining up to dance with you, Cole is going to wake up and realize what he could miss if he doesn't get off the fence. Neither one of us is suggesting you dress this way to train a horse or cook dinner. I certainly don't."

CJ thought for a minute as she looked at herself. The dress was peach silk with a scooped neck and thin straps. It skimmed her waist and flared at the hips till it ended in soft folds at her toes. Coral-polished toes that peeked out of a pair of cream-colored sandals with two-inch heels. The dress had a sheer jacket Hope had draped over her shoulders. She pushed her arms into the loose-fitting sleeves and pivoted, assessing herself in the mirror with a glance over her shoulder.

"If it was denim," she said, "and a bit shorter, I could get used to this."

Hope and Elizabeth sputtered then started laughing.

"Is that all you can say?" Elizabeth demanded when she brought herself under control.

What could she say? She looked like a princess but she didn't feel like Cinderella rescued from a life she hadn't been meant to live. Instead, she felt like an actress playing a part. It would be fun to see the looks on everyone's faces—especially Cole's—but she could only pray she could carry off wearing this costume and keeping up the masquerade for the night. Especially the high heels!

"I can't say I don't like looking like this, but it was so much trouble. Do you two actually go through all this? All the time?"

The two women dissolved into laughter again, and this time CJ joined them.

Chapter Sixteen

Cole had a plan. And his objection to tomorrow's race was at its core.

He didn't want to use Elizabeth as a shadowlike chaperon anymore. The longer he thought about CJ's assumption that she was only a stand-in, the less he liked it. What good did it do if he kept from breaking her heart but undermined her confidence in who she was? He liked who CJ was and, until he'd come along, so had she.

That was why he'd sent her flowers. So she'd know she was just as important to him as Elizabeth was.

One of the things he liked most about CJ was her inability to use artifice of any kind. CJ was a what-you-see-is-what-you-get kind of person. In the beginning her chambray and denim wardrobe had bothered him, as had her outspokenness, because he thought she was pretending to be as masculine as many people thought her job was. He'd quickly come to realize that CJ was exactly what she looked like. Her freshly scrubbed face, callused hands and rough-and-tumble wardrobe defined her. CJ was a grown-up version of a tomboy.

And so tonight, right after he made sure CJ knew how proud he was to have her on his arm, he would make sure she was so busy trying to keep him in line that neither of them would have time to think about kissing, touching or feelings.

He pulled to a stop in front of her cottage and took a deep breath. It wasn't good that his heart was pounding already. He hadn't even seen her yet. He felt as if a thousand butterflies had taken flight in his stomach, and they weren't even enfolded in the close confines of his car yet.

Then she opened the door.

Cole swallowed. ''CJ?''

She was a vision from his worst nightmare. His stupid delaying tactics—the ones that were supposed to guard her heart—had somehow destroyed every bit of self-confidence she'd ever had. She'd turned herself into an Elizabeth clone. For him.

This was very bad.

''Cole. Do you want to come in?'' she asked, her same sweet voice confirming that he was not seeing things. It really was CJ.

Stunned, nearly mesmerized and hating to admit that this CJ was even harder to resist than the one he'd been running from for months, he said, ''No. I don't think I'd better.''

Did his voice sound as befuddled as he felt?

"Excuse me?" she asked, a little frown creasing her perfect brow.

Luckily, CJ's confusion cleared some of his. "I mean we'd better get a move on. I don't want to chance getting as far as Graystone or Elizabeth's father in the receiving line and getting stuck talking to them because there's a logjam."

CJ glanced down at herself quickly, almost imperceptibly. "Oh. Then let me just get the jacket that goes with the dress."

He could tell CJ was disappointed that he didn't mention the way she looked. But he never did, because it didn't matter to him anymore. It once had, or so he'd told himself to counteract the attraction he'd felt for her when they met.

What he really wanted to do right then was scrub her face clean and throw his jacket over her nearly bare shoulders. Not because he didn't like the way she looked, but because she was even harder to resist. He didn't like what that said about him. Was he so shallow that a woman's appearance made this much difference to him?

He watched her walking down the hallway from her bedroom as she shrugged into a sheer jacket that unfortunately hid absolutely nothing. It was going to be a long night.

An hour later, the charity shindig in full swing, Cole approached CJ with not a little trepidation. He was lucky to have survived the ride to Graystone Manor with his sanity intact. At her place he'd thought once he had driving to concentrate on he would be able to get his rioting emotions under control. He'd been wrong. She wore a scent that reminded him of a pretty white flower one of his California partners had grown in his atrium. It had wrapped itself around him, driving him nearly insane all the way here.

He'd been so rattled by the time they arrived he'd let Graystone and Reginald Boyer corner him and talk him into being one of the emergency vets on hand at tomorrow's race. Until then, he'd planned to plead an emergency and not attend at all.

He could see CJ across the room chatting with his family and looking as if she belonged in their midst. Did she? Were the feelings that overwhelmed him when he looked at her the kind that would last a lifetime or were they as fleeting and artificial as her new look?

His gaze shifted to his sister. She had lent CJ the dress. Hope had not always worn clothing like that, but she had confided in him that she'd unconsciously hid her feminine side so Ross would be more accepting of her role on the farm. He was nearly sure that CJ hid nothing. She was—he grinned helplessly—the tomboy his sister had transformed for the night.

"So what do you think of CJ's new look?" Elizabeth asked from behind him.

Cole pivoted to face her and Jack Alton. Suddenly he suspected a conspiracy afoot, which was odd, since Hope had never been particularly fond of Elizabeth. He narrowed his eyes and watched her carefully. "What did you have to do with this? CJ never dresses like that."

Elizabeth made a hands-off gesture. "It's Hope's dress and shoes. All I did was stop by to make sure CJ didn't embarrass you tonight."

"I'd never be embarrassed by CJ," Cole snapped.

"Believe me, you would have died rather than walk in here with her dressed in a pair of velvet jeans and a silk shirt."

Cole gritted his teeth. "I wouldn't have cared. It might have made tonight easier. Did you ever think of that?"

He didn't wait for a reply but stalked away. Whenever Elizabeth took on that stuck-up debutante persona it annoyed him. But her message was clear. That was how practically everyone in this room would have acted had Elizabeth and Hope not intervened. Giving it no thought at all but that he wanted to show them all that he was proud to be CJ's escort, Cole strode up to her.

"Come on. Let's dance," he growled as he took her hand, leading her to the terrace area set aside for dancing. CJ went unresisting into his arms once they'd reached the darkened dance floor, and Cole took a deep breath hoping to calm down before CJ realized he was annoyed. Instead he stiffened, realizing he'd made a strategic mistake. CJ in his arms was a lot more dangerous than CJ sitting next to him in a car.

With her scent surrounding him and her compact

body so close to his, Cole wondered how things could get worse. Then he looked into CJ's luminous, golden eyes and found himself dipping his head to kiss her enchanting lips.

This, this is worse than just having her in my arms.

She was heaven and hell all wrapped up in one neat package. His fondest dream and his worst nightmare. The perfect woman for him had come into his life at a time when he was still unable to handle a lifetime relationship. And if he couldn't force himself to make a commitment to CJ, he suddenly knew he never would. Because when he thought of forever with her, he got a knot in his stomach the size of Philadelphia, and he didn't have a clue why.

"Is something wrong?" she asked when he lifted his head.

"Why?"

"Well, I admit to not having any experience at this sort of thing, but are you supposed to kiss me then look as if you want to chew nails?"

What could he say? *You tempt me beyond reason. You make me do things I've sworn not to do. I want to give you everything and I have nothing to offer.* "You're right. You're not very experienced," he said, and straightened, looking over her head and trying to pay attention to the rhythm of the music so he wouldn't think about the woman in his arms and the hurt look he'd just put in her eyes.

After that number, the music switched beats. He took her back to the family, then excused himself on the pretext that he saw a fellow vet and had to co-

ordinate the next day's animal emergency team
with him.

Instead he went for a walk in the darkened gardens
surrounding Graystone Manor. They matched his
mood perfectly. And there he made his decision.

He had to cut CJ out of his life. It was the only
way to keep from continuing to hurt her. But he
couldn't leave home. Not again. This was where his
roots and his family were. His father might drive him
crazy, but he loved him. And the family was grow-
ing. He didn't want to miss that. Cole was a sucker
for kids, and it was beginning to look as if he
wouldn't have any of his own. But he could at least
enjoy his little brother or sister and niece or nephew.

He wasn't sorry about the move to Lonesome
Valley. Amelia deserved privacy with her new husband and baby. But it had given him a greater ap-
preciation for his family. The problem was, even if
he moved Mischief to one of the stables at Lonesome
Valley, he would still have to cut his professional
ties from Laurel Glen's farm operation to avoid contact with CJ. And that would be too obvious. CJ
would know she was the reason and she would quit.
Something she could not afford to do.

Cole decided he would go to his father and tell
him how uncomfortable CJ made him. He would offer to pay a full year's severance for her if his father
would fire her. That way CJ could get on with her
life, and he could get on with his, with no shadow
of unfulfilled possibilities staring each of them in
the face.

Cole was on his way to the party, determined to finish out the night, when he ran into his father. "Son, I'm glad I caught up with you. I wanted to say thanks for cooperating about the event tomorrow and for coming tonight. But don't you think you're carrying it too far holding meetings about the emergency team tonight? Forget all that and have a good time. If you don't get in there and dance with your date, some other lucky guy's going to steal her right out from under your nose." Ross laughed. "CJ is having the time of her life, and so are all her dancing partners."

Jealousy, hot and acidic, burned inside him. "Actually, Dad, I wanted to talk you about CJ. I have a favor to ask. I need you to let her go."

"Go?" Ross asked, clearly not understanding.

"As in fire her. I'll put up a year's severance pay so she can get herself established somewhere else. Or…or maybe we could find her another position somewhere else first. That would be better."

"Why would I do that? Why would you want me to do that? Don't tell Hope I said this, but CJ's a better trainer than your sister. You want me to reward her for all her hard work by getting rid of her?"

"I know it sounds crazy, but it's either that or I have to break my contract with you. I can't work with her anymore."

"What? This makes no sense. Anyone with half an eye can see she's crazy about you."

"Exactly. She's getting too attached to me and—"

His father's jaw tightened. "That's what this is about?" he snapped. "You and women. You don't want to leave them alone, but the minute they come to care, you want them out of your life. Well, not this time! CJ is a valuable member of Laurel Glen."

Cole bristled. "And I'm not, is that it?"

"I can replace you as our vet in about five minutes by calling the vet group, but a trainer like CJ comes along once in a lifetime. After how long it took to find her, I can't afford to give her up."

"Five months ago CJ Larson was a stranger you didn't even want to give a chance. Now your son is asking you for a favor, and you're more loyal to her. Thanks, Dad. I finally know for sure how much I mean to you. Please see that your precious trainer gets home. I have an emergency to see to."

CJ stood in the shadows trying to hold in the sob that clawed at the back of her throat. If tonight was supposed to push Cole over the edge, it certainly had. It must've been obvious to him that she'd dressed to please him, so he'd asked her to dance. Then he'd kissed her.

As before, his kiss had transported her to a different plane. It had been just as immediately clear that whatever the kiss had been about, it had not been a gesture of love. She had somehow disappointed him. After that, he hadn't wanted to be near her. She'd gone looking for him to ask him for an explanation. Now she had one.

Not one to run from confrontation, CJ stepped out

of her hiding place and into Cole's path. So many conflicting emotions battled to the surface, but she went with anger. He would not see her cry.

"CJ." He stared at her, clearly horrified.

"I just want you to know, I'll start looking for another position immediately. But keep your severance pay. I don't want your money. What I wanted, you apparently can't give."

"That's exactly what I've tried to tell you." The anguish in his voice was too real to be an act. "I told you the day after Morning started to recover. I told you, I don't *do* love. I told you I *can't*. I wanted you to leave for your good, not mine. You came here tonight looking like an Elizabeth or Hope clone. Somehow you got the idea that the way you dressed—the way you *are* is the problem. You're perfect the way you are. Or were. The problem here is *me*. I don't want to be like this. I just *am*. I've tried to change but I keep finding myself right back here pushing someone who cares about me away."

"I feel very sorry for you. I don't know why you want to live your life so alone. I hope you wake up and look around you and see all you're missing before it's too late."

CJ was thankful the next morning was Sunday. After a mostly sleepless night of tears and lonely thoughts, CJ went to church and prayed for guidance. She tried to listen to His direction during praise and worship but it was harder than ever before. Maybe because she'd thought the Lord had spoken to her when she'd been given the opportunity to work at Laurel Glen. For a while, it looked as if she'd heard Him. Now she wasn't so sure. And for the first time in her life, she couldn't seem to hear God's voice. CJ was alone in a way she had never been before, and she had never felt such despair.

The worst part of the situation was that she'd come to think of the Taggerts as family, and now her presence was tearing that family apart. Ross had been wrong to choose her over his own son, even if he thought Cole was wrong. CJ was, after all, exactly what Cole had said—a stranger.

After church, CJ went directly to the Graystone cross-country. The atmosphere was one of anticipation or tension, depending on where you walked. If you were near the grandstands, the attendees were anxious for the event to begin, but if you wandered through the rows of trailers it was clear the participants were unsettled and nervous.

"Ross," she called, finally finding him after checking nearly every line of trailers at Graystone. "I need to talk—"

CJ stopped. Ross looked up from where he was sitting on the rear bumper of the trailer. She had never seen him look so terrible. Even Ross's Prize seemed to know something was wrong. The big stallion shook his head and pawed the ground, restive and agitated.

"What on earth is wrong?" she asked, moving to shield Ross from the hot rays of the sun.

"I have what has to be the worst headache of my

entire life. There's no way I can risk Prize by trying to ride when I feel like this. Especially not that course. The trouble is no one's going to believe anything but that I walked the course and knew we couldn't handle it. It looks as if Cole's going to get his way. Would you trailer Prize while I go scratch us?''

This was just plain wrong! CJ knew Ross was right. The only explanation that would appear in the sports section tomorrow was that Prize had been scratched at the last minute. People would draw their own conclusions and, human nature and rumors being what they were, Laurel Glen would be hurt by this. It would have been better not to enter at all. And to add insult to injury, Cole had warned them, and that just plain made her furious!

"Oh, no. Cole is not going to get his way," CJ said. "Not about this, anyway."

Ross got to his feet. "I heard you confront him in the garden after we argued. CJ, I'm so sorry. I don't know what's the matter with that son of mine. And don't think I'm going to let you leave because of him. I have a year's contract, remember."

"Ross, listen to me. I have to leave. Cole is family. I'm not. One of his biggest problems is not feeling like part of your family. But I think an even bigger problem is his relationship with you. You shouldn't have chosen me over him. He's your son."

"But don't you see? I know he loves you. If you leave, he'll never admit it. I only refused to let you go for his own good."

At that moment, CJ would have loved it if Cole were there. That way, headache or no, she could have knocked their heads together! "So, instead of telling him that, you told him he was easier to replace than me. How was he supposed to know you were keeping me on for *his* good? You're as bad as he is. He told you the race was too dangerous for your horse rather than tell you he was worried about you. Do you see a pattern here?"

CJ smiled and wished she had a camera to prove the formidable Ross Taggert could still blush. But her smile faded when Ross leaned against the trailer and dropped his head against its steel wall. He groaned.

"Are you all right?"

"Besides being an idiot, you mean?"

CJ couldn't fight the grin that tipped her lips at the corners. Ross and Cole might spend a lot of their time battling with each other, but they shared the same dry sense of humor.

"Besides that, yeah. Look," she said in the take-charge voice she used on only the most recalcitrant of her charges, "forget about the race. Take Amelia and Meg and go home. I promise to tell everyone I see that you took sick suddenly. After I do a little damage control, I'll see Prize gets home safely."

Ross sighed. "Thanks. I may stop by the med tent and load up on aspirin before we head home."

CJ watched Ross leave, then, after eyeing the stallion, she set out to disobey her boss.

Chapter Seventeen

Cole finished taping the six-year-old hunter's knee and straightened his stiff back, wiping the perspiration off his forehead. Graystone had picked the perfect day for his torturous little event. It was hot enough to fry an egg on the hood of any car in the parking lot. And the humidity was right up there with the temperature.

Of course, it wouldn't have been a good day for him no matter what the weather was. The encounters last night with both CJ and his father in Graystone's garden gnawed at Cole. He hadn't slept. He hadn't eaten. He was barely functioning.

Cole knew he'd finally done it. He'd pushed CJ so far away that there was no possibility of a future for them. That was supposed to have given him a feeling of relief. She was mad, not brokenhearted. Instead he felt hollow and alone.

Sleep had stubbornly refused its silent ministrations. It had remained a distant goal throughout the night. Then he'd begun to torture himself, wondering how to get back the place he'd lost in his father's heart. After which, the hurt of Ross's rejection made him wonder why he even cared.

In the distance, Cole heard the announcement calling Laurel Glen's entry to the start line, and his stomach rolled. Angry as he was at his father, Cole still worried about him.

"Jerry," he called to the other emergency vet on duty. "I'm going to take a break and watch Prize run the course, or as much of it as I can get into position to see." He sighed and shook his head. "Sometimes I wish I was the parent. I'd have grounded him for this."

"Go," Jerry ordered. "I wouldn't want to be in your shoes today. Say a prayer we don't wind up with any more casualties of Graystone's summer insanity. Next year I think we should organize and take him to court to stop this."

"I hear ya," Cole called over his shoulder as he walked into the August heat. Absently, he wondered why his hackles no longer rose over the idea of being told to pray for something. Time was when Jerry would have gotten a lecture on the futility of prayer.

Seconds later he saw the flash of someone running toward the starting point and realized it was his father. But Ross wasn't dressed to ride in an event. He was bareheaded and wore a T-shirt and jeans. Cole sprinted forward and called to him, wondering what was going on. Ross looked back but shook his head then kept running.

By the time Cole got to where the start banner hung, the starter pistol had launched the next rider— the Laurel Glen rider—onto the course.

"If you're here, then who's riding Prize?" Cole demanded when he reached Ross's side seconds later.

Ross pointed toward Prize and the rider taking the first in a series of hazarded jumps but didn't look away. "CJ." Ross puffed and sucked in a breath.

Cole's eyes shot to where his father's gaze fell, and he saw a thick golden braid streaming from beneath the helmet the rider wore. He felt sick, afraid and too many other awful things to catalog. "Have you lost your mind? You let CJ ride for you?"

Ross shook his head but said nothing. He kept watching CJ's forward progress, his hands fisted at his sides.

Cole found he couldn't stand to watch. And he suddenly understood. His fear of commitment was all wrapped up in an event that had happened half a lifetime ago. He'd been afraid he'd lose her the way he had lost before. Not to someone else. But to death. And now he just might. He looked away, and fury raged to the forefront of his emotions.

"Wasn't having one woman die in the dust because of you enough?" Cole asked, his teeth gritted to hold in the fear.

His father turned to face him then, and Cole bit back a gasp. He'd never seen Ross Taggert so pale.

The pain in his eyes was physical, and clearly had nothing to do with Cole's remarks. Ross opened his mouth, but no sound came out, then he reached for Cole and crumbled into his son's arms.

"Dad!" Cole yelled as he eased his father to the ground. Curious onlookers crowded around them, and Cole shouted for them to get back. Several clear-thinking people pushed the others away, and he asked one of them to alert the pilot of the helicopter on standby in a nearby pasture.

The event's emergency team, a couple of local paramedics who'd been circulating through the grounds watching for signs of heat exhaustion in the crowd, rushed up. They thought they were dealing with simple heat problems. But there had been something in the way Ross had looked before going slack in Cole's arms. After Cole explained that he was a veterinarian and that he was afraid his father might have had a stroke, they called the hospital for instructions. When Cole heard how dangerously high Ross's blood pressure was, he knew his concern had not been unwarranted.

Operating on automatic pilot since Ross's collapse, Cole realized his young, vibrant father's life could be in danger. There was no way Ross was flying off alone in the care of strangers. Cole told the paramedics exactly that, then stood.

He looked around, knowing the family was in the stands, but he couldn't spot them. As he ran alongside Ross's stretcher, he grabbed his cell phone and called Jeff. He told his brother-in-law what had happened. Jeff promised to get hold of Aunt Meg, who was with Amelia, and all four would meet them at the hospital.

Cole climbed aboard the helicopter, then the steady whop-whop of the engines quickened and the craft lifted off. After he buckled his seat belt, he checked his watch. Had it only been a little over five minutes since Ross's collapse?

Then a thought sneaked into his mind on cat feet. *CJ's still riding the course.*

He looked down as they flew low over Graystone and saw her taking a series of downhill jumps. His heart leaped into his throat when Prize skidded sideways and nearly fell as they entered a water hazard. He could tell CJ had barely held on.

He'd heard about this year's nightmare course from several of the riders and he'd seen the damage done to a couple of hunters who'd run early on. There was no way Cole could convince himself CJ wasn't in danger. It was like watching his mother climb aboard that black stallion again. He hadn't thought to ever feel such terror a second time.

Cole twisted in his seat to keep her in sight but lost her when the chopper rotated and sped toward the hospital.

CJ slid to the ground at the finish line. Her legs felt like rubber, and Prize staggered, as muddy, wet and exhausted as she was. Cole had been right, she thought as she checked Prize for any obvious damage. Charles Graystone *was* a maniac. The stallion didn't seem to have suffered any injury in their near fall toward the end of the course. She thanked God for His protection, but she also asked forgiveness for not investigating the event well enough and for letting her anger at Cole goad her into riding for Ross.

As she led Prize toward the rows of trailers, CJ stopped and glanced at the standings, but her score wasn't yet posted. She didn't care if she'd won or not. This hadn't been about winning. She'd ridden out of anger, but she'd also ridden for the Taggerts and Laurel Glen, to show that the farm had come back from all its problems with good stock and an outstanding training program.

Shaking her head in disgust, CJ turned away. It was time to take care of Prize. She needed to get him washed down, fed and rested before she loaded him into the trailer and headed home. She patted the big stallion's neck as they slowly made their way to the trailer.

About an hour later, CJ was resting in the shade of the trailer when she heard her name called. She opened her eyes and yawned, looking around. She'd only just gotten to her feet when Elizabeth and Jack Alton rounded the front of the trailer. Both looked terribly grave.

She stood. It was apparently time to start facing the music. "I know. I know." She defended herself before either of them could launch into her. "Riding for Ross was a little out there. Actually, considering the course it was a lot out there, but—"

"CJ." Elizabeth cut in. "Didn't you hear? Ross

collapsed right after you started the course. They used the standby helicopter and flew him to the hospital. Cole went with him.''

CJ dropped onto the chrome running board of the pickup. "He had a terrible headache so he decided he couldn't ride. But he didn't complain of anything else. He said he was going home."

"Well, he must have come back, because from what I hear, he collapsed near the start line right after you took off. My father says he thinks Ross and Cole were arguing."

"All those two ever do is argue," Jack Alton said.

Elizabeth stooped, took CJ's hand and put a set of keys in her palm. "Take my car and go. Cole will need you there."

CJ shook her head. "No. You and Hope were right about last night. It did push Cole over the edge where I'm concerned. He wants me out of his life. Last night in the garden I heard him ask Ross to fire me."

Shaking her head, CJ stood and handed Elizabeth the keys.

But Elizabeth was having none of it. "You take these back," she ordered, plunking the keys in CJ's hand again, "and get yourself to that hospital. My car is at the entrance to the trailer lot."

CJ looked at the keys. She should explain that running the cross-country was her idea and that Ross knew nothing about her decision. And then there were Hope, Amelia and Meg Taggert. All three women had been more than kind to the newcomer in their midst. She should tell them her prayers were with them and Ross.

"All right," she conceded, "I'll go, but I need to get some of this mud off me first." She held her arms out and displayed her grubby clothes. "I doubt they'd let me in the front door this way."

Cole paced the hall outside the waiting room. The whole family was in there praying, and he felt like a caged tiger. He was worried about his father and nearly frantic to hear if CJ was all right. He wanted to throttle both of them. Apparently, his father had been warned about his high blood pressure over a year ago but had not been back to the doctor since. And Cole was furious with CJ for riding in the cross-country when she hadn't trained for it.

The worst part of the whole thing was that if Ross died the last words between them would be harsh ones. Inside his head all he could hear was CJ saying, "Talk to your father. Tell him you love him. Tell him you're sorry. Don't wait too long. Don't wait too long."

Had he? Had he waited too long? Was this the way it would always be?

Cole heard footsteps and walked up the hall to meet Jim Dillon, the pastor from the Tabernacle, the church the family attended. Initially, Cole had been pretty uncomfortable around the young pastor who moonlighted as a carpenter. When Jim had worked on a handicap-equipped kitchen for Jeff, before he regained the use of his legs, the pastor had kind of grown on Cole. Jim didn't preach his beliefs. He said he just lived them and answered questions when asked. In that way, CJ was a lot like him.

"How's Ross?" Jim asked.

Cole shrugged. "We don't know anything yet. They're running tests and such," he told the pastor, motioning toward the room where the family still prayed.

The young pastor looked into the room and shook his head. "It looks like they're talking to Someone far more helpful than I can be. You, however, seem to be all alone. Why don't you go in and join them? Prayer can move mountains."

Cole dropped onto one of the long benches that lined the hall. "Last time I tried that my mother died, anyway."

Jim nodded and joined him on the bench. "It happens that way sometimes. Since we don't know all the things He knows, sometimes it feels as if He doesn't listen. Me, I pray for God's will."

"Huh?"

"I pray the way Jesus did in the garden the night before He died. Not my will but Thy will be done. And I pray for the strength to deal with His will. Because you see, He never promised anything but that He would be there for us to help us through hard times."

Cole thought back to all the talks with Granny Taggert and recalled her saying much the same thing. So had CJ in their conversation about free will. Now he was hearing the same thing from Jim Dillon. Why hadn't he remembered it sooner?

"I was a Christian once," he said suddenly. "But I doubt God would want to hear from me again."

"I hate to shock you, but it's sort of a once a Christian always a Christian thing."

Cole shook his head. "I've been pretty vocal against any form of religion or faith for years."

Dillon shrugged. "And Peter denied Christ three times. They'd been the closest of friends. Our God's the forgiving sort when we repent. Just ask Him. The chapel's thataway," he said, pointing down the hall, then he stood and went into the waiting room to join the family.

Anxious and haunted by the memory of Ross collapsing in the middle of their argument and of his last glimpse of CJ running the cross-country, Cole stood and paced. Some minutes later he found himself standing in the aisle of the little chapel. It was as if his feet had carried him there without checking with his brain. He looked up at the cross, and a sense of peace fell on him like a blanket.

"I'm sorry," he said aloud. "Sorry for the things I said. Sorry I didn't make peace with him. I'm sorry I pushed CJ so far away with my blind stupidity that I'll never get her back. I'm just so…sorry." He trailed off, choking back tears that fell anyway. It felt right suddenly to kneel before the cross and ask for the strength to handle whatever came next, but it also felt right to ask that Ross not only live but recover to be the kind of father to his new child he had been to Cole and Hope. He also prayed that CJ was safe, even if she couldn't be with him.

Cole understood that there might be a bigger plan he couldn't see, but at least he had asked. And the Person he'd asked had the power to make his prayer reality.

Chapter Eighteen

Cole looked up as Amelia sank into the pew next to him. "Did—"

"Everything's fine," she told him and gave him a quiet little smile. "Jim Dillon thought I might find you here."

"He was pretty confident of himself," Cole replied without rancor, sliding backward into the spot next to her.

"He was confident of *you*. So am I. So you've finally made your peace with the Lord?"

Cole nodded.

"Good." She put her hand on his where it rested on his thigh. "Now suppose you try for two out of two. Your father's awake. You were right. It was a stroke complicated by heat exhaustion."

He dropped his chin to his chest and closed his eyes to hide his tears. "I don't think I ever wanted so badly to be wrong. I was arguing with him when—''

''Now you hush,'' the steel magnolia at his side ordered with a squeeze of her hand. She stood. ''The doctor has credited you with Ross's *good* condition. Fact is, so far they don't think there was any appreciable damage. And his doctor says that's because they had him here so quickly. He's doing so good he's up there shouting down the ICU and already driving his nurses crazy. Seems he wants his son and won't take no for an answer.''

Cole stood, too. ''Then we'd better get a move on.''

Amelia gave him a faint smile. ''ICU is on the third floor. I have something of my own I have to tend to right now. You run along without me. I just left him, and Meg is in there.''

As Amelia moved away from him, Cole realized her gait was a bit slower and more strained than it had been these last few days. Could all the excitement and worry have brought on labor? She was due soon. ''Amelia,'' Cole called as she stepped into the hallway. ''What floor is labor and delivery on?''

Amelia froze and turned to him. ''You think you're pretty smart, don't you?'' She propped a hand on one hip. In her advanced stage of pregnancy her annoyance lost itself in the translation. Cole could only grin at the picture she made.

She glared. ''And if you say there isn't much difference between a pregnant woman and a pregnant mare I swear I'll clobber you.''

Cole chuckled as Jeff and Hope came down the hall. "Here we are," he said taking Amelia's arm. "These two can use this as a dress rehearsal." He tried to keep it light despite the lousy timing. "I'm off to see Dad, you two. And Amelia is off to have his baby. Would you guys escort her there before she tries to do something brave like have this baby alone?"

"Amelia! Dad would have our heads," Cole heard Hope exclaim as he turned and rushed toward the elevator.

His first glimpse of his father didn't quite match Amelia's enthusiasm. Nor Aunt Meg's. Cole had just passed her in the hall. He supposed it was the contrast to the usual vibrant Ross Taggert that was so upsetting. His father certainly looked better than he had when he'd collapsed.

Cole had known there would be IVs and monitors, but seeing his father hooked to them once again brought home to him how fragile life was.

"Dad? Are you asleep?" Cole whispered as he entered the room. His father was not shouting the ICU down. He was lying in the bed with his eyes closed.

Ross's blue eyes popped open. "Just resting my eyes, waiting for you." He didn't say anything for a long, uncomfortable moment, just stared at Cole.

Cole didn't know what to say. He wanted to clear the air and apologize for his part in their estrangement. But was it safe to get into the years of misunderstandings and strife between them? Before he could decide on a safe topic, Ross grimaced and looked away.

"I really messed up," Ross said gravely.

"What made you think you could ignore a warning of high blood pressure with all that went on with Donovan and the damage he did to the farm?"

"I don't guess it would be a good idea to tell a medical man that maybe I thought I could control my own body. But that isn't what I meant about messing up. That was just plain stupid. I know that now. I've had more lectures since coming to than a room full of delinquents.

"I mean I've messed up with you. CJ was only too happy to point out what an idiot I am when I talked to her this morning. Son, I wasn't choosing her over you last night. I hoped if she stayed on at Laurel Glen you would finally admit your feelings for her. If it hadn't been for you, I might not have followed Amelia in time to catch Donovan that day he monkeyed with her car. Without discovering him where he shouldn't have been, I never would have known she was in danger. A minute later, and I'd never have caught up to her in time to save her. It seemed the least I could do for you was keep the woman I knew you loved nearby."

Cole shook his head, starting to deny his feelings. Not because he didn't have them, but to save face because he was sure he'd lost CJ forever.

"I've seen the way you look at her," Ross said. "I'm in love, too, and I'm not blind."

Pressing his lips together and fighting embarrassing tears, Cole nodded then took a deep breath, reaching for composure. "Well, thanks for the thought, but I'm afraid I destroyed any chance I had with CJ.

"While we're in apology mode, though, I'm sorry I didn't say I was worried about you running the cross-country instead of getting on my soapbox about the danger to the animals. *And* for what I said at the start line this morning. I know Mom's death wasn't your fault. It was a cheap shot, bringing it up like that. But watching CJ ride onto that course…" He bit hard into his bottom lip, but it didn't help. He scrubbed his eyes with the backs of his hands, still wishing he knew how she was. "I wish you hadn't let her—"

"But I didn't know," Ross told him. "I went home and left her to scratch Prize. She was supposed to bring him home after she did some damage control about the scratch."

"Then what were you doing back at Graystone?"

"Jack Alton heard CJ had substituted herself as the rider because I was under the weather. He called to see how I was and offhandedly mentioned that they'd let her substitute for me so I shouldn't worry. I'd walked that course." He took a tired breath. "Not worry? I got back there as quickly as I could, but I was too late to stop her. I never wanted anyone to take that kind of chance for me again. I think what got my blood pressure so high in the first place was seeing what Graystone had in store for all of us. Truthfully, I thought about scratching Prize before I got the headache. I'm ashamed to say it was pride that stopped me. I hated to admit you were right. Again," he added, the tremendous pain of the past evident in that one little word.

"Because I've never stopped rubbing your nose in what happened the day Mom was killed."

Ross shook his head. "It's a hard thing for a man to admit he made a mistake in judgment that took a life. When that life is the man's wife, the woman he loved, the mother of his children, it doesn't take anyone to remind him, son. The fact that I ignored your warning about the horse just made it that much harder to live with."

"Yeah, well, I let Donovan use me back then, and that couldn't have made things any easier. I guess Amelia told you he was part of the problem between us."

"Son, you were a kid. Don't blame yourself for listening to a manipulative adult bent on revenge. He did the same thing to me. I think there's been entirely too much guilt and blame between us for years."

But Cole wasn't going to let himself off the hook so easily. "You made a mistake. I deliberately set out to destroy both of us. It might have been a crazy kid thing to do, but I still did it."

Cole looked at the cold tubing that fell over his arm when his father grabbed his wrist. It was a chilling reminder of how close they'd come to losing this chance. "And I've still refused to let you forget those mistakes. You came home an accomplished adult trying to put peace between us, and right from the start

I pushed you away. I finally saw what I was doing, but by then I'd alienated you all over again. There's one thing I want you to know. I'm proud of you and all you've accomplished. You're a good vet and an even better man. I'm proud to call you my son.''

''I've always been proud that you're my father.''

CJ strode into the hospital lobby and went right to the information desk. ''Hi, I'm hoping you can tell me where I can find the Taggert family.''

''Taggert,'' the gray-haired woman behind the desk muttered absently as she ran her finger down a computer listing. ''Well, now. It's been a busy day for Taggerts. Which one are you looking for?''

''I understand Ross Taggert was flown here from the Graystone cross-country,'' CJ replied. Were there other Taggerts in the area?

''Ah, yes. ICU. Third floor, left off the elevator.''

CJ turned to walk away, but curiosity and worry got the better of her. ''Excuse me,'' she said to the woman. ''Could you tell me the name of the other Taggert admitted?''

The woman smiled. ''Amelia Taggert is on the second floor. Labor and delivery.''

Minutes later CJ emerged from the elevator on the second floor. She wandered a while before finding Hope and Jeff in a sunny waiting room. ''I came as soon as I could,'' she said, entering and holding out her hand to Hope and clasping it when she reached her.

Jeff stood. ''*You* are in big trouble.''

CJ held up her free hand traffic-cop style. "There's nothing you can say to me that I didn't say to myself on that course. I kept expecting it to get a little easier or at least even out a little."

"But it never did, did it?" Jeff grumbled. "I rode once in the Graystone at my father's insistence. Once is all it took."

"How's your father?"

"He's going to be fine," Hope said, her relief a palpable thing. "Cole's with him now. Aunt Meg is in with Amelia. The two of us are going to take turns as her coaches."

Backing toward the door, CJ forced a smile. "Good. That's great. I just stopped by to let you all know my prayers are with you."

"Where are you going?" Hope demanded.

CJ shrugged. "This is a family time."

"And you're family," Hope protested.

"No. *Cole* is family, and last night he made it clear he didn't want to be around me. I think I embarrassed him, trying to be someone I'm not."

"And I think you shouldn't make assumptions," Cole said from behind her.

She hadn't heard him come in and whirled to face him. His face gave nothing away, allowing her no hint as to what his cryptic remark meant. His intense gaze shifted from her to his sister.

"Kitten, somebody has to tell Dad about Amelia. I was thinking it might be better if it comes from somebody in a, uh, similar situation."

"In other words you chickened out."

Cole winked. "Got it in one, sweetheart. I'm not about to test my newfound relationship with him by telling him he has to stay up there while Amelia's down here delivering his baby."

Hope stood and shook her head. She walked out resolutely, followed by Jeff, who clucked like a chicken and elbowed Cole as he walked by.

Cole chuckled. "You know it, brother," he said with a laugh in his voice. He sobered when they were alone and his gaze fell on her. "I don't know what to say to you, CJ. I've acted like such an idiot since the moment we met, and you deserve an explanation."

"Cole, it's okay. Really." She pivoted and walked around him, but he curled his fingers over her shoulder just as she stepped into the hall.

"Please. Let me explain. I know it's too late for us, but you need to know this for you."

Us? CJ hardened her heart and turned, crossing her arms protectively across her chest. He was not sucking her in again. "Fine. But I don't need to have my inadequacies cataloged by you."

He shook his head. "It's *my* inadequacies we're talking about here." Cole's slight grin was clearly self-deprecating. "So this could take a while. Would you come back in and sit with me? Let me explain?"

Completely confused, CJ allowed herself to be led to a sofa at the far end of the room. She studiously ignored the feel of his touch and how handsome he was. Cole sank to the sofa a cushion away and turned to face her. She could feel his gaze and sneaked a glance at him but refused to give in to the temptation of looking into his compelling eyes. Instead, she turned and stared straight ahead.

After a few moments Cole sighed and said, "Okay. Just as long as you listen. I once told myself that if I ever met a woman like my aunt or my sister I'd run in the other direction. I thought it was a joke, but it was probably the most truthful remark I've made in years. That, in a nutshell, is what I've been doing since the day I met you."

CJ didn't understand. She refused to look at him. Her last glance at him had been enough temptation, with his hair askew and the sunlight glinting in it. If she looked into those dark-chocolate eyes she'd be lost. She just knew it.

"The only similarity between me and the women in your family is our love of horses and our faith," she said tiredly. Why was resisting temptation so hard?

"Your faith makes all four of you very special women. And very unusual. And don't think I'd have been running out of aversion. One of my big problems with you, from the beginning, was my attraction to you."

Now she was really confused, and she finally turned to look at him. She blinked. He looked so unhappy. Dare she call it heartbroken? "You're attracted to me? I don't understand."

Cole chuckled, but it was a mirthless sound. "No, I don't suppose you do. For the record, I knew there was something different about the way you made me feel from the moment I first saw you. For a long time, I thought I was guarding my heart. When I moved back here from California, I had myself convinced that what I lacked with the women I've dated was the ability to trust them not to hurt me the way I thought my father had hurt my mother and then later the way I knew she had hurt him.''

''Don't you know I would never hurt you?''

He stared at her for a few seconds, then he pursed his lips and nodded. ''Oh, yeah,'' he whispered hoarsely, then cleared his throat. ''I figured that out a while ago, once I got to know you. And then I thought I could try to build a relationship with you, but I was afraid by that time it was me who would hurt you.'' He shook his head and made a disgusted sound. ''Not an unfounded worry, the way things have turned out.

''CJ, this is the part you have to understand. I tried to use Elizabeth as a sort of warning flag for you. I told you I didn't do love, but I was afraid you'd still think you could change me—reach my heart. So I've kept her between us. I didn't know if I'd be able to commit to building a future, and I didn't want you counting on me too much.''

''Then Elizabeth really is just your friend?''

He nodded, and raked his hands through his hair. ''But it backfired, and that's why I need to tell you all of this. I realized that you were starting to lose confidence in yourself because of the kind of woman Elizabeth is. So I tried to show you I *was* attracted to you. But I still didn't tell you the truth about her place in my life."

CJ fought a smile. How ironic was that! "You didn't care that I don't fuss with myself and wear expensive clothes the way Elizabeth does."

"Exactly. The problem was I still didn't understand what kept me from committing. I got a knot in my stomach even thinking about a lifelong future with you. Now that I've finally figured it out, I'm sure it's too late. But you deserved to know why I've put you through what I have.

"This morning, when I looked up and saw you riding onto that course, my mother's death flashed through my mind. And, between one breath and the next, I knew what the fear was all about when I thought of us and a future."

"Oh, Cole."

He shook his head, clearly not wanting her sympathy. "I've spent a small fortune on therapists trying to figure this out, and all it took was facing exactly what I was so afraid of." He took her hand, and she finally looked him in the eye. He was fighting tears—actual tears—over the thought of losing her!

"What were you afraid of?" she asked even though she could see the answer written in his tortured expression. Her heart pounded, and CJ realized Cole wasn't the only one seeing through a veil of tears. He'd said it was too late for them. Didn't he know it was never too late for love?

"I lived in terror that I would lose the woman I

love. That she would die and leave me all alone again. I looked up and saw you riding onto that killer course, and I felt the same way I did watching my mother climb aboard a horse I knew was dangerous. And I felt the same way I did after every time I've held you or kissed you. It suddenly all made sense.''

"Now what?" she wondered.

He shook his head and wiped his eyes with the back of his hand. "I wish I knew. I love you, but is saying it enough to wipe out all the hurt my vacillating has caused? Should it be? Personally, I think you deserve more. And I think I'm a pretty lousy risk.''

Her heart in her throat, she asked, "Do you still want me to leave Laurel Glen?"

He looked absolutely stricken. "No! I never wanted that. Try to understand. I'd just danced with you. Held you. Kissed you. And I panicked. And there you were looking like a princess. All dressed up, trying so hard to please me. Trying to be what you thought I wanted because of the way I'd used Elizabeth. And I still couldn't be anything you needed. I thought if you left you could build a new life, and I could stay near my family without having to watch you go on without me.''

"If you don't want me to leave, then what *do* you want?"

She'd known that under all his charm and lighthearted quips he had been troubled by the past, but the near desperation carved on his features told the real story of his inner struggle these last weeks.

"You. I want you and your love," he said, the words a broken whisper in the room.

CJ tilted her head and smiled through her tears. "You have it. You've had it for weeks."

But Cole, it seemed, would never react the way she thought he would. Rather than gather her into his arms, he shook his head and turned away to slouch down on the sofa. "But I don't deserve it. Don't you see? You should be...courted."

"Courted?"

"I know that's an old-fashioned word but I don't think there's a modern one that fits. We should go out to dinner. The movies. Picnics. Church."

"Church?" Now she was really confused.

"Uh. Yeah. Remember you told me there are no atheists in foxholes? I discovered there aren't any in hospital waiting rooms, either. I'd been thinking for a while on and off about God and Mom's death, but I kept telling myself I had time to think some more. I was wrong." He grimaced. "I seem to spend a lot of my time being wrong. Then Jim Dillon showed up here today, and something he said just clicked."

"Well, I think it's wonderful that you finally turned your heart back to the Lord."

"Actually, so do I. It was like having this weight lifted off my shoulders and my heart. I still prayed that Dad would be all right, but I knew if he wasn't, I had another Father who would see me through. I wish I'd turned to Him when we lost Mom. It all would have been so much easier."

She nodded. "Cole, about dinner and the movies

and such. We did all that. If you count the play. I'm
not the kind of person who cares if someone spends
money on me. We spent a lot of wonderful time
around the horses and playing with Dangerous.
We've had dinner once a week with your family.
Dating is about getting to know each other. I *know*
you.''

"I mean you should be courted with the prospect
of marriage in the future. I was so afraid, when I
thought about the future, that the special times we've
had together have been tainted by me pulling back
and hurting you. I know I don't have the right to ask
for a second chance—"

"Do you want a chance?" she hastened to ask.

He blinked and sat up, clearly startled. "Of course
I do."

"Then it's yours. And so am I."

His smile, for the first time, held more than a hint
of shyness. "You are?"

"Yep," she said, and went to him as he finally
gathered her into his arms.

Epilogue

Cole turned in his saddle and smiled as he watched CJ slide to the ground out of Morning's saddle. God had been so good to him. CJ was everything he'd ever wanted, even if he'd been too thickheaded to recognize it. Thank God, and he constantly did, that He had sent CJ into their midst and that Ross had kept her there.

This last month had been like a dream. First, Amelia's baby had been born in record time. But before the blessed event, Aunt Meg had somehow convinced Ross's doctor that bringing Ross down in time to see his daughter being born would be less a strain than missing it.

Cole was glad the baby had been a girl. Not because he was afraid a son would have displaced him with Ross but because his father was so gaga for the tiny little Laurel. She already had him—and everyone one else at Laurel Glen—wrapped around her miniature pinky.

Ross had continued to show such rapid improvement that he came home only days after Amelia and the baby. And Laurel Glen was doing incredibly well, too. CJ's win at the Graystone cross-country had done what Ross had hoped. It had reminded old clients of their promise to return their business to the farm once the problems were solved. His father had been right about that, but when CJ was interviewed about the win, she'd made comments that had a good many people looking carefully at the legitimacy of the event and weighing the dangers it presented.

About the only thing that hadn't gone right was that Jim Lovell seemed to have disappeared off the face of the earth. Cole had called Lovell's superiors looking for him and had been stalled, put off and downright ignored. Jack Alton might be working out as a foreman, but his air of mystery and his interest in Elizabeth still had Cole worried. He shook his head, trying to banish negative thoughts. Jim was a big boy, and he'd get in touch when he returned. Cole had to learn to be patient.

At any rate, it was too beautiful and clear a September day to waste time on worries. The sky was bright blue with fluffy nimbus clouds floating across the horizon. It was the perfect kind of day for a picnic.

In the last several weeks he'd planned a multitude of outings for CJ, but she seemed to enjoy nothing as much as she did a picnic and communing with nature. He'd decided that this hill above Lonesome Valley would be the perfect place to bring her today.

Today was a special day. He wished he knew why he was so nervous. He knew CJ loved him. She told him as often as he told her how much he loved her. But Granny's diamond ring, wrapped carefully in his pocket, added gravity to the next step in the old-fashioned courtship he'd planned for CJ.

"Oh, I love this view," CJ yelled over her shoulder to him as she reached the crest of the hill. "I just wish it didn't have such a sad name."

Cole threw his leg over Mischief's neck, slid to the ground and walked to stand behind her. He cupped her shoulders in his hands and dropped his chin on her head, loving the silky texture of her golden hair against his skin.

"I had a dream about this place back when my grandparents were still alive. And I made a promise to Granddad to make it come true one day. I saw this place the way it must have been at one time. Brimming with life. Filled with laughter and happiness. That was before Mom was killed and everything fell apart.

"For so long afterward, I put this place out of my mind and heart. But the first time I brought you here the dream came slamming back to me, and I knew I still wanted it. I just didn't know how to reach out and make it happen."

He turned her to face him and reached blindly in the pocket of his jeans for the ring, unable to wrest his gaze from her beautiful golden eyes. "I swore to myself I wouldn't rush this with you, but I can't wait to live the future I was so afraid of before.'' He took her left hand in his. "I know I'm no bargain. And that sometimes I have all the tact of a raging bull, but I love you and will till the day I die. Charity Jane Larson, will you marry me and make me the happiest man on earth?''

CJ huffed out a breath. "I never thought you'd finally have enough of this stupid courtship. Now put the ring on my finger and kiss me."

Colt put the ring on her finger as ordered and scooped her up in his arms, kissing her while fighting jubilant laughter. He had a feeling there'd be a lot of laughter in the house below in the years to come. He knew there'd be a lot of love.

* * * * *

If you enjoyed
MOUNTAIN LAUREL,
you will LOVE the
next story in Kate's exciting
LAUREL GLEN series:

HER PERFECT MATCH

by Kate Welsh
On sale January 2003

Don't miss it!

Dear Reader,

I hope you enjoyed this third book of the LAUREL
GLEN series. I've waited anxiously to write this book,
because Cole and his perfect match and polar opposite,
CJ, were actually the inspiration for this entire series. But
Cole's story had to wait. And wouldn't you know it was
the toughest of all three to write—isn't that just like him
to give me trouble! Then, though I'm happy to report it,
researchers have come up with a vaccine to prevent West
Nile virus in horses.

The reason this book was so much trouble—other
than Cole just being Cole—is that I had to come to
the same place Cole did about the Lord. I had to
answer Cole's questions for myself so I could answer
them for him. He didn't understand how a just God
could let terrible things happen. He had to learn that
the exercise of free will changes lives and that if God
were to constantly intercede, He would, in effect, be
taking away a precious gift—the free will He's given us.
Cole also had to discover the reason bad things happen to
good people. Without a believer's viewpoint, he couldn't
see that our Father in heaven knows what is beyond our
pain. To God the leap from life to death is only one step
because He can see our reward on the other side. And He
can also see that here on earth life goes on and those left
behind, though they grieve, survive and go on with their
lives until it's their turn to leap.

So are you wondering what's happening with
Jim Lovell out in Colorado? And have you figured out
who Jack Alton is? I'll answer those questions and more
when the rest of LAUREL GLEN series comes your way.

God bless you.

Kate Welsh

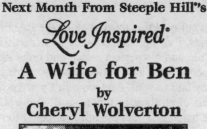